ALSO BY K.B. DIXON:

Andrew (A to Z)
The Sum of His Syndromes
My Desk and I

A PAINTER'S LIFE

A NOVEL

K.B. DIXON

PORTLAND • OREGON
INKWATERPRESS.COM

Copyright © 2010 by K.B. Dixon

Cover and interior design by Masha Shubin

Cover illustrations © 2009 JupiterImages Corporation.

www.inkwaterpress.com

ISBN-13 978-1-59299-448-9
ISBN-10 1-59299-448-2

Publisher: Inkwater Press

Printed in the U.S.A.
All paper is acid free and meets all ANSI standards for archival quality paper.

1

For Sandra Jean

A Painter's Life

1

Christopher Freeze was born rather undramatically in Phoenix, Arizona—at the time a city in transition: a sprawling, major-league-sports-franchiseless nowhere in the middle of the Sonora desert that was fifty years and who knows how many millions of gallons of illegally diverted river water away from becoming the wealthy golf and retirement Mecca it is today.

A relatively healthy baby, Christopher endured the usual cavalcade of childhood maladies: chicken pox, mumps, whooping cough—usual with one significant exception: hospitalizations at the ages of nine and eleven for stomach ulcers, the product, it was professionally surmised, of pathological worry.

(EXCERPTS FROM THE UNPUBLISHED JOURNALS OF CHRISTOPHER FREEZE)

Back in the studio this morning. I wanted to pick up where I had left off on *Untitled*, but I couldn't. I couldn't make myself care about it—not in the right way. All I could do was sit there and stare stupidly at those first 100 strokes and wonder what it was that had gotten me started, what it was that made me think I knew where this was going. It's probably another terrible idea and I just don't know it yet. I'll try to get a little distance, to rejoin it, to fix it, but I won't be able to. I'll slap at it and slap at it and slap at it again—who knows how many times—before I give up and scrape it down, before I say to myself at the end what I am saying to myself now: that it's another mistake, another waste of precious time.

❖

It is a difficult thing in these early hours not to feel trivial—or, feeling trivial, to carry on.

❖

David Andres was saying if he could just get the right people to object to something of his, to insist that it be removed from wherever it had been placed, it would be the making of him. It would mean a reputation, which is money in the bank. It would mean a better bottle of wine with dinner, a car with more horsepower, a house with more square feet, a girlfriend with fewer cats.

❖

Ran into Aaron Powers at Downtown Drugs. I haven't seen him in a couple of months—not since we showed paintings together at a charity auction for the Library. He is growing a beard. It's probably a good idea because he has been cursed with a completely uninteresting face. I told him it looked good. He said thanks, but from the way he said it I could tell he wasn't really comfortable with the thing, that he felt like a bit of a fraud—like a bald man wearing a hat. Anyway, I was looking for toothpaste, and Aaron was after some sort of new herbal concoction he had read about somewhere because he was afraid he was coming down with something. I hate it when you run into someone and they tell you they think they are coming down with something because when they tell you that you have to stand there, make concerned faces, and talk to them as if nothing was wrong when what you really want to do is jump back a couple of feet and say sorry about that, but whatever it is, don't give it to me. I especially want to do that because I am one of those people who lives in terror of getting something—no matter how small—because no matter what it is, if I get it, I get a bigger, more unpleasant version of it than other people. I don't get sick easily, but when I do get sick, I get very very sick—and it is not just my physical reaction that is extreme, but my emotional one, too. It's a sort of double whammy— extra sick and extra depressed.

❖

Safadi's is not a gallery—it's a menagerie. I fit right in.

❖

I received a letter today from someone named

3

Alan Barnes. I have never heard of him before, but from his handwriting—which is a little overly scrupulous for my taste—I imagine him to be another shifty, middle-aged art history professor with tenure issues and a weakness for underaged blondes. He is about to begin work on some sort of profile or monograph, and he was wondering if he could pay me a visit. I can tell from the pro-forma nature of the request that he isn't really wondering at all—he already knows the answer. He just wants to get my rejection on the record. He probably thinks it will help him make a point.

Sarah and her tan—it's a complex relationship that a paleface like me couldn't possibly understand.

(EXCERPTS FROM VARIOUS REVIEWS)

"A sort of on-again/off-again complex-style surrealist, Freeze works in that sparsely populated corner of the genre reserved for slumming skeptics.

Temperamentally his pictures are reminiscent of Soutine's. But the simply drawn figures, elaborately stuccoed surfaces, convoluted, idiosyncratic resolutions—these are uniquely Freeze's."

4

2

When Christopher was seven his family moved into "the big house" on Flower Street where he became a builder of forts, radios, and smoke bombs. He took violin lessons (briefly), spent hours with his microscopes, constructed model rockets, and over time put together a small menagerie that included rabbits, pigeons, lizards, and gerbils. Once he got a bicycle he was almost impossible to keep track of. There were several mishaps involving fire—one that led to the inadvertent burning down of a billboard advertising Volkswagens. There was a preternaturally athletic girlfriend named Lauren, a best friend named Connor, and at the age of fourteen, there were two long nights spent in a juvenile detention facility.

(Excerpts from the unpublished journals of Christopher Freeze)

I like my pictures to look crowded—sort of stuffed into the frame. The canvas should be full like your plate when you sit down to dinner—suggestive of emotional and/or metaphysical abundance.

❖

I don't want to be part of the perpetual revolution, the chasing after novelty. The freedom to go where you want is one thing, but the obligation to move on, move on—that is the demand made by a policeman. You are never saying anything; you are trying to say it. You never get to finish or to amplify a thought.

❖

Another night arguing with my lumpy friend Brian Stark. I almost never agree with anything he says, but I like listening to him try to say it because he has a downright mesmerizing way of talking out of both sides of his face. A certain amount of this is to be expected when you're trying to put things into words that can't really be put into words, but Brian is positively chronic. If I caught his drift—it's always difficult to know for sure given his backpedaling and perpetual circumlocution—he is worried right now that he is getting set in his ways, that the stuff he likes is not cutting edge enough. It is a sign that he is ossifying, that he is becoming simple-minded or right-winged (implied difference is his). He is against any painting that is in any way easy to like. He sees this as pandering—except, of course, when he doesn't. This or that is always good and bad—except some of the bad has goodness in it and some of the good has badness in it. He likes it, finds in it a surprising and formal richness, except for certain dreamlike quali-ties that have no real significance and appeal to those who have no actual interest in being enlightened. It's always like this with Brian—the sound and fury of contradictions signifying nothing. He wants things as many ways as he can have them. He lives in abject terror of being pinned down, of being proved wrong—or worse, bourgeoisie. He will never let a characterization of his position on a picture go unchallenged. He will always insist your understanding of his understanding is fundamentally flawed. He is very touchy for someone who tries so hard to seem casual and easy-going.

❖

Sarah wants to talk tonight when she gets home. She wants to sort some things out—things about the way I have been acting lately, things she understands the ramifications of much better than me.

❖

Bought a new ergonomic studio chair that is supposed to help with my back. It has all sorts of adjustments—levers, buttons, knobs. The instruction manual is as fat as a phone book.

❖

Got into one of those not particularly engaging conversations about religious issues with James Ransom the other day. Our subject was the book of Genesis. I told him it was all very interesting, but for me the world began with the Kennedy assassination—or

7

maybe it was when the Beatles appeared on *The Ed Sullivan Show*.

❖

I hate watching people look at my pictures. I never like anything about the way they do it.

❖

I fell in love with the magic of shadowing early on, and I have never felt the need to be subtle about it—in fact, just the opposite. I like to call attention to it. The magic is itself always part of the subject for me.

❖

Coffee with Lewis Moore. Haven't known him all that long. A still life painter, he got tired of the hard time he was having in New York so he moved out here, found a small place in the Pearl, and started letting himself go. Says he has put on fourteen pounds and developed a television habit—that he lives on *Perry Mason* reruns and pizza. He still hears from his old friends—one in particular named Zachary is trying to talk him into moving back. He says it would be better for Lewis as an artist and a person to live in New York, but Lewis isn't interested. He says he likes living here. Says the Mayor was just arrested for drunk driving—or should have been. The fact that he wasn't has gotten a lot of people upset. He wants to stay around to see how things work out.

❖

I can't imagine what led Barnes to settle on me. I know the big guys have been done and done again and that for quite some time now these profilers, monographers, biographers have been forced to pin their hopes on obscurer and obscurer middle-sized guys, but have they used them up too?

He is going to find me tremendously disappointing. I have never been interested in being interesting—not in a way he would like, not in a way that would make life easier for him. There are no betrayed mistresses to unveil, no famous friends, no hidden homosexual adventures, no bad behaviors caught on the front page of anything.

(EXCERPTS FROM VARIOUS REVIEWS)

"Color is obviously an issue for Freeze. He seems unapologetically attracted to the guileless dazzle of the jewel tones. While not committed unreservedly to being pretty for pretty's sake, he is not afraid to indulge an inclination when it presents itself."

9

3

Samuel Johnson once complained about being the child of older parents, saying that one became "the plaything of their dotage." As the child of parents who were too young, the opposite was the case for Christopher. From early on he was left pretty much to his own devices as his parents were preoccupied with a plethora of private dramas. Christopher's father, William, did what apparently most fathers did at the time—invest himself in affairs and in efforts to get richer—while his mother, Margaret, after providing breakfast, lunch, and dinner, disappeared into neurosis and alcoholism.

Freeze's early interest in art was feeble—it consisted mostly of an insatiable demand for ever larger boxes of crayons and an inclination to finish entire coloring books at a single sitting.

It was in college where people first started to describe him as withdrawn and moody.

(EXCERPTS FROM THE UNPUBLISHED JOURNALS OF CHRISTOPHER FREEZE)

Too literal a transcription bores me. I require a

certain amount of deformation. It can be very little or a great deal—right up to the point of complete abstraction. But at that point—the point of complete abstraction—my interest starts to head the other direction, away from the work.

❖

Portland Art Dealers annual gala was held last night at the Hilton. Showed up late as usual; grabbed a drink as usual; found Colleen's little crowd as usual; and started drawing up a list of people I wanted to avoid. Jeffrey Nicholson was right there at the top. Jeffrey is a freelancer. He has said some nice things about my pictures, but I can't stand the guy. Tall, skinny, head shaped like a wedge of cheese—he is one of those not-so-gracefully aging bad-boy types. He thrives on this stuff—on parties—and thinks they are a reason for living. I watched him with a repulsed fascination as he worked the room—sort of the way you watch an iguana. He seems to have some sort of internal clock that tells him when it is time to move from one scrum of fashionables to the next. I have no such clock. If I find myself in a conversation I stay in it until it dies an awkward death. Then I head for the bar.

❖

My signature may not be legible, but that doesn't mean my paintings aren't.

❖

11

If you want to calculate the true distance of any trip, you have to multiply the miles traveled by the number of people in the car.

❖

With Brian it is all about being an insider, about getting the jokes and the allusions. There is something to admire about his single-minded dedication to contemporary stuff. It probably has something to do with his having been raised by wolves. He doesn't get bored nearly often enough.

❖

Rare run-in with Donald today. What does one make of a man who still—after all these years—talks to his dead mother? How desperate was he to be loved and what does it say about my callousness that this desperation seems to me so pitiful?

❖

I don't insist on a third dimension, but I'm not afraid of it.

❖

Met Mark and Kevin at the Virginia Café for lunch. Kevin was preoccupied with the Wicks thing. (He is teaching full-time now in Shield's department and would like to give that up for painting full-time. He sent his portfolio over to Wicks a couple of weeks ago and is waiting to hear back.) Mark, on the other hand, was preoccupied with Hannah Miles—Kevin's much put-upon inamorata. Being successfully ensconced in what appears to be a long-term liaison with the irrepressible Sophia White, Mark feels compelled to pass out lots of free relationship advice. He thinks Kevin—who is a committed shilly-shallier when it comes to this sort of thing—needs to consider getting seriouser about Hannah. He is certain Kevin's continued caution will be his downfall.

❖

Had a long talk with David Minot about finding a PR person. He is an enthusiast; I am not. For one thing, I have no interest in going through the preliminaries of meeting with X, Y, and Z—of selling myself and my work to whomever. I wouldn't object to making a few more dollars (I am going to need them if I am ever going to have a chance to develop a taste for the finer things in life), but I would object to the guidance that came with the opportunity. Ignoring all those well-made arguments would be exhausting—the energy better spent painting pictures.

❖

Am under the impression that Dr. Hatcher is having problems with his wife. I can't quite put my finger on what they are, but a sense of them—that they are many and serious—has seeped out from under the questions he so artlessly asks me about Sarah, about the constancy of my sense of her, about her reactions to the burdensome incarnation that is presently me.

❖

I wonder who will talk to Barnes and why? The people who know me know I don't want any part of this sort of thing. They can and will for the most part resist his blandishments I suspect. It's the people who don't know me or know me only a little or dislike me who will have things to say. What sort of record is that likely to provide?

(EXCERPTS FROM VARIOUS REVIEWS)

"It may seem quaint in this day and age (when it is, in fact, quaint to use the word 'quaint') to suggest that an artist's first test is draftsmanship, but let me suggest it and let me say that as a draftsman Freeze is superb."

(EXCERPTS FROM VARIOUS INTERVIEWS)

DL: I was wondering if you came from an artistic or visually oriented family?

CF: No, I don't think you could call them "artistic" or "visually oriented." What I came from was an olfactorily oriented family. My father claimed he could smell electricity, and my mother was always telling us how many hours it had been (plus or minus a quarter) since this or that person had bathed or showered. I myself am similarly sensitive. The stench of the studio is one of the things I like best about being a painter.

DL: But you obviously have an aptitude. Did this separate you from your family?

CF: Well, I was definitely separated from them—but I don't think it had anything to do with artistic aptitude. Maybe it was artistic temperament. I had lots of problems and concerns—none of which I felt inclined to share. I feel sorry for my parents. They missed out on having a regular son. I don't think they thought about it much, but it's really what they wanted. Instead of having a regular son, they had an irregular one who they didn't understand—an irregular one who wasn't really the least bit interested in them.

4

As money started to move into Phoenix so too did a desire for not only new and better golf courses, but for new and more prestigious educational institutions from which the fit and rich might graduate their ungrateful offspring—hence the founding and funding of Campbell College, a sort of pint-sized Dartmouth in the desert.

Freeze spent his first semester at Campbell in a dormitory near the Language and Literature building. Finding his roommate, the food at the student union, and the communal bathrooms distinctly uncongenial, he moved as soon as he could into a small studio apartment about a half-mile from campus where he lived for the next three years on coffee, cheese, and raisins. Except for playing pool with his friend Dan Mahalick and the occasional romantic dalliance, Freeze kept pretty much to himself—reading, drawing, and going to the movies as the spirit moved him.

(EXCERPTS FROM THE UNPUBLISHED JOURNALS OF CHRISTOPHER FREEZE)

It's almost impossible to be funny or ironic in a

painting. Many have tried, but few have succeeded. Those who have succeeded have only succeeded sort of. They've been funny (to some degree) or ironic (to some degree), but none of the resulting stuff has been wholly first rate. It is the great misfortune of this medium: to do reasonably good work in it one must be earnest.

❖

I've started talking to a girl at the coffeeshop—the one who usually takes my money, not the one who fires off the espresso machine. Her name is Michelle— the one who takes my money. She has curly hair, huge eyes, and what they used to call an "alabaster" complexion. She is a strange girl—in part, I think, by design. She clearly indulges her anomalies. Mostly it works, but there are times when you get the feeling that some things about her aren't quite for real.

Anyway, one of the local landscaping crew was leaving the place just as I went in this morning, and the smell of him led Michelle and me into a discussion of smells in general—and, in particular, the smell of new-mown lawn. For Michelle the smell of new-mown lawn is the smell of summer; for me, it is the smell of servitude and misery. I told her about those terrible times as a child when I was compelled to spend 100-degree weekends mowing my grandmother's lawn—a thickly thatched thing roughly the size of a football field. For me that smell—the smell of cut grass—was the smell of back-breaking manual labor, the smell of heat, the smell of salty eye-stinging sweat, the smell of low energy levels, the smell of spiritual exhaustion, the smell of despair.

This comment about the "smell of despair" led us into a discussion of despair in general (there is lots of it out there right now)—and, in particular, into a discussion of a man named Peter who lives in Michelle's apartment building. He used to be filled with despair, but now he is filled with serotonin uptake inhibitors and seems just fine—except for this fantasy he has started to nurture about Michelle and him having some sort of future together. (Apparently he has a recurring dream where Michelle comes downstairs late at night, knocks on his door, asks to come in, and then confesses that for quite some time now she has been watching him out at the pool and that she thinks the muscles in his back are the most beautiful she has ever seen.) Michelle says her roommate, Liz, thinks the medication has made Peter unattractively sensitive (according to Michelle, Liz's taste runs almost exclusively to firemen). Michelle says that she personally has no objection to a man being sensitive—just so long as he keeps it within reason.

She wanted to know if she had ever told me anything about her roommate's aquarium. It seems just the idea of it is keeping her awake at night. Her recurring dreams—such as they are—are now almost always full of fish.

Dr. Hatcher is a heroic sufferer of headaches. We commiserate with abandon.

❖

What am I trying to do with this picture? I'm trying to bring back something I knew in the night—something essential and elusive, something that has gotten away, but not that far away.

❖

It's always fun to listen to Brian's complaints about others as they are so often mirror images of others' complaints about him (mine included). One of his favorite words is "meaningless"—something is always this or that, "but meaningless," which, of course, is exactly the way most of us would describe a conversation with Brian.

❖

Another talk with Safadi about pricing my pictures, about finding a balance. Very depressing. I need some money, but I just can't think about paintings this way—not productively. I end up doing what I always do, which is leave the calculations up to him and hope for the best.

❖

Sarah and I have started referring to Kevin and Hannah as Mr. and Mrs. Doppelganger. They've been duplicating our getaway weekends to Cannon Beach for a while now. When they go, they stay where we stay, eat breakfast where we eat breakfast, buy an ice cream cone where we buy an ice cream cone, buy a book where we buy a book, and take the same walk on the beach that we always do (down to Haystack Rock and back). We could understand them trying it out once or twice perhaps because we are always talking about this routine of ours (not just as an escape, but as a pilgrimage to a certain psychic place from which we draw strength and comfort—a private religious practice, if you will), but they have probably repeated it a half-dozen times now, and we have started to see this act of mimicry as plagiarism. We are wondering if maybe we can sue.

I understand Barnes has been to both Westside and Grove, that he has seen files, and that he has tracked down several classmates with memories of who knows what. Will he wonder why I was never in the school play, why I was never in student government? What about sports—my foray into little-league baseball, my sprinter's speed, those ridiculous shorts I had to wear at that last track meet. What about the grades I got in Geography—what is he going to make of those? What is he going to make of my single visit to summer camp and my prolonged fascination with Apaches? What sort of insignificant scrap will he unearth—a book report, a teacher's comment on how nicely I played with others, a note in the back of somebody's yearbook. A nothing to make something out of. Beware the academic in search of his Chapter 1.

20

A PAINTER'S LIFE

(Excerpts from various reviews)

"There is an extravagance to Freeze's pictures. Feeling is plastered on the canvas with a palette knife—the vast forehead of 'Uncle Ray' is a whirlpool of slathered umber icing."

5

Although Freeze had sketched and doodled in a haphazard way since high school, he first began to take these efforts seriously under the generous tutelage of a professor by the name of Thomas MacIntyre. A moderately successful painter in his own right, MacIntyre taught an introductory class at Campbell called "The Fundamentals of Art" in which he spoke inspiringly about form, line, shape, value, texture, color, and space—and about art as a way of life.

Professor MacIntyre, his wife Katherine, his son and daughter Brad and Kit, quickly became Freeze's second family. He visited them frequently, had dinner with them maybe twice a month, and slept in their study on a shaggy goatskin rug when he got too drunk to drive home.

(EXCERPTS FROM THE UNPUBLISHED JOURNALS OF CHRISTOPHER FREEZE)

I like Derrick Thomas, but I have always been a little suspicious of him. As a human being he seems happier than he should be. He positively bristles with charming quirks.

❖

I get all my best ideas in the shower, which is one of the reasons I take so many every day (four or five at least). It means heavy hot-water bills and dry, itchy skin, but you do what you have to for a picture. It always comes first.

❖

I am thinking about doing a series of pieces that look like the work of an unmedicated schizophrenic—vivid, illogical, horrifically detailed pieces depicting the compulsive pursuit of a merciless exactitude. I've done a couple of sketches and I'm still not sure. There is something deeply satisfying about a crazy patch done right, but pure, unadulterated hallucination is a bore for everyone I think. The trick is to make the unreality real so the beauty at the heart of this particular species of otherness can be revealed.

❖

A call this morning from my dentist's office. They think it is time for me to come in and have my teeth cleaned, but I don't. They think I should come in every six months, and I think it should be more like every six years. We are working on a compromise.

❖

Looked over and there was Sarah smiling at me—calm as a cat.

❖

Before Michelle moved here she lived in Santa Monica. She supported herself (just barely) giving tennis lessons at the Brentwood Country Club to uncoordinated women with rich and restless husbands. She says she was pretty good back then, that she had been captain of her high-school tennis team, and that she had once beaten Stephanie Kirschnick in a divisional quarter-final (Stephanie Kirschnick who turned pro, who was once ranked 134th in the world, and who was beaten [6-1, 6-1] by Venus Williams in an opening-round match at the 2002 Canadian Open). Michelle had nine students—not one of whom was athletic or teachable. The basic ground-strokes were one thing, she said, but working with these women on their serves—well, that's what drove her out of the business.

❖

I've never understood playing solitaire. Wasting time alone is like wasting money.

❖

This new picture should work. I keep trying to find out how. I've tried it this way and that way and several other ways as well, but none has been right. I know it exists—a way—and when I find it, it's going to seem easy and commonsensical and I'm going to wonder what took me so long. Then, of course, shortly thereafter I'm going to start to wonder if I am sure—maybe it seems easy and commonsensical for a reason: because it is. If it *is* easy and common-sensical—rather than just *seeming* easy and common-sensical—then it's wrong and not "the way" either. Where will I go from there?

❖

I can't help but wonder about Hatcher's professional life. How did he get to where he is today; how many full-fledged psychotics does he have on his books—violent people, frightening people, people who require massive amounts of medication. What do the rest of us look like to him in comparison?

❖

The thing most often overlooked when assessing a still life is pathos. Virtually all of the best are bathed in it. The subtly transmitted sense of compassionate sorrow will never be fully explicable, but is related to the missing element—the human element—and the basic existential story that is implied.

❖

Funny thing about manners—you don't really think about them until you run into someone who doesn't have any.

25

❖

Clarkson is focusing his new work on boredom. He isn't trying to make it interesting—he is trying to make it legitimate. If he can make it legitimate, there is a chance it could catch on and become this season's sexy.

❖

Kevin says he and Hannah have started talking about moving in together. Mark, the Raj of Romance, will be thrilled.

❖

It seems Barnes has found some early drawings. It won't take him long to manufacture connections to my mature work—to find in these juvenile scratchings the proto- or embryonic-expressionist.

What is he going to make of my college years where the opportunities for misinterpretation increase exponentially? He will tie me to someone with whom I have no ties and then speculate about their influence—a teacher, a writer, a painter. He will come across a name that will lead him to another name that will lead him to another name—and similarly with conclusions, from one to another to another as he whittles me down to size. He will make me wish I had been pleasanter and more cooperative. What conclusion will his readers come to in the end but that they were better off not knowing me? And who am I to argue? I have to at least suspect that this may be true.

How will their knowing this me—the me concocted by Mr. Barnes—affect their subsequent assessment of my pictures?

(EXCERPTS FROM VARIOUS REVIEWS)

"Freeze's paintings—which have a strong, rapidly-executed look—suggest a commitment not only to the considered or deliberately developed image, but to the aesthetic of the spontaneous. His pictures seem, at least in part, unmediated transcriptions. In the quick, sketchy, gestural application of paint—in the ooze and goop and flicking brushstroke of it—he has recorded a set of visual reactions that are distinctly individual."

6

Eager to study art in the flesh and not just in reproduction, Freeze started making regular trips to the Phoenix Art Museum where he became slightly obsessed with what was at the time their only good picture: a Carlo Dolci painting titled *Salome with the Head of John The Baptist*. Freeze did a group of paintings that were variations on this theme and showed them at the student gallery. This show produced his first review. It appeared in *The Bridge*, a student newspaper, and was titled "No Disappointment." The reviewer was a young man named Bruce Richardson. He found the work to be "a Baroque interpretation of a cubist Catholicism." Richardson went on to become the art critic for *The West Side Weekly*, an alternative paper, where he spent several satisfying years taking shots at David Column, the regular critic at the local daily, for his knee-jerk inclination to laud the trendy and his hideous, ham-handed prose style. Richardson later wrote a small book about William Dyas Garnett, a teacher, painter, and muralist who died, as so many have, without getting the recognition he deserved.

Professor MacIntyre counseled his young protégé

to pursue graduate study—the idea being that on completion of this degree Freeze might join the Campbell faculty. Eventually Christopher did consider graduate study, but not at Campbell. He needed a change of scenery. He was tired of the heat and the horticulture. A little fishing around by departmental muckity-mucks produced an offer from Greenhurst, a small liberal arts college in Portland, Oregon.

(EXCERPTS FROM THE UNPUBLISHED JOURNALS OF CHRISTOPHER FREEZE)

Mornings like these, when it is gray and rainy and things are going lousy and I'm feeling all sorry for myself, I can't help wondering what it would be like to be free of this compulsion—to be happy doing something else instead of being whatever it is I am being now doing this.

❖

A piece in *Pearltown* about Roberto Penaloza and his show at Rubino's has Brian, the crown prince of the colloquial contradiction, wound up and spewing his usual—as in "sorta great, but vapid."

The piece by Thomas Wygant is one of those opaque, polysyllabic waxings about essences and cosmic connects that Penaloza gets greeted with these days, and it has driven Brian not quite over the edge but close enough to it to feel the breeze.

Penaloza's work—a sort of contemporarified Abstract Expressionism—is a rough-drafty looking mix of paint and personal calligraphy. Things are crossed out, quasi-erased, smudged. For me there is something fun about the scribbling, but I don't think there is anything profound about it. His pictures are easy things for people who like to read things into things to—well—read things into. They are struggles for something—allusions to the vitality of chaos decorated here and there with the exploding splodge.

Penaloza's stuff is normally the sort of stuff Brian loves, but he is annoyed by the prices and the incessant praise Penaloza has been getting, and he has decided to have reservations. He has decided there is something wrong with the later work; that Penaloza's new stuff looks too much like his old stuff; that he is, in fact, impersonating himself. He also holds Penaloza responsible for the crap that is being written about him. He thinks Penaloza encourages it.

Safadi's assistant, Colleen, was married to a painter named David Ford. They were divorced several years ago and began a long, strange, post-divorce relationship. They lived in a sort of limbo (more than friends, but less than man and wife) until Colleen decided it was time to move on and David was left to pretend he was taking it in stride. She got remarried just a couple of months ago to a man named James Cooper—a large, big-boned, square-headed man—a cabinetmaker who almost always smells a little of shaved wood.

❖

If one wants to truly challenge the established notions of what art should be, they should challenge the idea that it can be anything. But, of course, if you do that you will find yourself labeled a philistine—at which point the debate is magically over. It's as if there was an "alacazam," and you disappeared.

❖

Coffee with Aaron and his new beard. Apparently he has been on a mission to make himself more attractive to women. He has been working on his "look" and on pretending to be a nice guy—on smiling more. He wanted to know what I thought of his voice—was it low enough. It seems he is thinking about taking lessons to improve it.

❖

Safadi is negotiating a deal with Anthony Spencer for *Winter Disturbances*. I've asked him to keep me out of it. Details about that sort of thing depress me.

❖

Kevin is an unusual sort of teacher. He doesn't want to be everyone's friend, but he does want to show everyone a certain amount of respect—if not as an artist, then as a human being. There are easier guys at Greenhurst—lots of them—and a few who

31

aggrandize themselves by being bastards. Kevin falls into a confusing middle category.

❖

Couldn't sleep. Tormented by solutions to the café picture. None of them any good.

❖

I have—against my better judgment, but at Sarah's request—agreed to meet with Barnes. I wonder what his first impression will be—physically, I mean. I'm sure he knows what I look like, that he has seen a photo somewhere, but this is going to be our first face-to-face; he is going to have his trusty little notebook out, and there is going to be something about me that surprises him—something that seems radically different from what he was expecting. Hopefully he is one of those poetic embellishers. I remember that thing Friedman wrote about my hands—about my "long, elegant fingers." They are not long and elegant—they are regular hands and regular fingers, but for strategic reasons it seemed important to Friedman that his readers think otherwise. It would be nice if Barnes were aiming at the same sort of hogwash-loving audience, but I don't think he is.

(EXCERPTS FROM VARIOUS REVIEWS)

"There is a curious mix in Freeze's pictures—a not always decipherable blend of object and sensation.

Everything is close-up, brought forward, impatient—its essential spirit pressed right up against the picture-plane."

7

Freeze arrived in Portland with the rain, which started in September and didn't stop again until July. His faculty advisor was the crown jewel of the Greenhurst Art Department: Ethan Shield.

Shield, who was born and raised in the middle of the Midwest and who had, like most ambitious young men of his time, moved to New York to make a name for himself, had been living in Portland for several years—hiding out from his reputation and a series of ex-wives.

Shield and Freeze hit it off right away. In addition to an amused suspicion of the world in general, the pair shared a number of artistic interests—the most peculiar being a mutual, almost fanatical, admiration of Rubens. While in most contemporary circles it was considered vulgar—almost criminally unsophisticated—to respond to this sort of flamboyant virtuosity, Shield and Freeze idolized the painter as something of a wizard in courtier's clothing—Freeze inspired by his vigor, Shield by his variety.

Freeze's reaction to Shield's work was complicated. He did not care for much of the early stuff.

It seemed too desperate to be at the front of a new generation of under-30's and, with its decorative use of superfluous esoterica, its play on cuneiforms, hieroglyphics, and runes for example, too eager to be thought brilliant. But he marveled at the later work where Shield began to forgo this sort of showing off, where he simply focused his remarkable powers of observation on what was in front of him—pieces like *State Fair*, impossibly complex and still somehow so straightforward you could smell the excitement and taste the cotton candy.

(EXCERPTS FROM THE UNPUBLISHED JOURNALS OF CHRISTOPHER FREEZE)

I don't think of my pictures as small—I think of them as efficient.

❖

The story of the Impressionist has been the central one of my painting life. It is not the direction they took painting that has proved their most significant contribution—it is the direction they took criticism. Critics have never really recovered from having gotten it so wrong. They lost their authority, their courage, and their audience. No one pays attention to anyone anymore who isn't simply gushing about how wonderful this or that thing is. As a consequence, the infamous herd of "independent minds" is never thinned. There is lots of good work out here, but it gets lost in the crowd. The first job of a painter now is not to paint—it is to get noticed.

❖

The trouble with Thornton is that when he gets an idea he pounds it like a tambourine.

❖

Sarah is always trying to sort things out among our friends—organize them into groups. There are those who like us more than we like them, those who like us less, and those who seem to like us equally. Among those who like us less than we like them are some we would like to like us more and some we are happy to have like us the amount they do. Among those we like less are some we think we should probably be liking more and some we would just as soon went away. Among those who like us as much as we like them are some who could easily end up in one of the above categories and some (our best friends) who no matter what happens are destined to remain exactly where they are.

I think she made a chart.

❖

Michelle has promised not to tell me any more dream stories. They're not the sort of thing you would characterize me as being naturally receptive to. She is going to save them, she says, for the hazelnut latte drinkers.

❖

Spent an hour looking at a new Kinsley picture –*The Sleeping Dancers*. It's big and beautiful and one of the best things I've seen in I don't know how long. I found myself wishing I didn't know as much as I did about Kinsley though (for instance, that he is a religious fanatic—a cultist) because it kept getting in the way of my experiencing the thing. I found myself becoming suspicious of its simplicity—wondering if what I took to be a charming allusion to innocence might not be a cynical pandering to the theological base.

Woodson said he would like to see it. I told him it was worth the trip down to Salem, but if he was going to do it, he had better do it soon before Kinsley sent it off to his dealer in Texas.

❖

Sophia thinks there should be a certain amount of drama in a relationship—turmoil like she sees on television. Mark, a pragmatist, obliges her when he can. They argue regularly, they hang up the phone on one another, they stomp out of restaurants. Somehow, though, they seem careful never to take it too far.

❖

I am meeting Alan Barnes tomorrow for coffee. What should I wear? Whatever I choose I'm sure it will be duly noted when he recreates the scene. "I first met Freeze at the Happy Monkey, a coffeeshop not far from the Safadi Gallery. He was dressed casually, as you might expect—wearing jeans, tennis shoes, and a sweater"—that sort of thing.

How much did I weigh? What were my hobbies? Where did I ever get the idea that I could make a living as a rattlesnake rancher? (The allusion is to a comment made in an interview last year.)

Who will I be sitting there across the table from this man—certainly not me. I'll be someone else, someone babbling about who knows what—someone trying to be real but not succeeding.

(EXCERPTS FROM VARIOUS REVIEWS)

"Clocks are to Freeze what apples were to Cezanne. He arranges them with both formal and thematic consideration. In one painting you find them huddled together like homeless people on a freezing night, destiny scrawled across their antique faces; in another they are spread laterally to form a sort of skyline, a city made of time. Some pieces are compositional free-for-alls—scale changes, dimensions meld, the relationship of background to foreground shifts, light comes from one direction, then another, then another. The invitation to explicate and hypothesize is unmistakable."

(EXCERPTS FROM VARIOUS INTERVIEWS)

GH: How much time do you spend in the studio?

CF: Quite a bit. It's very frustrating that so little of it is productive.

GH: What sort of preparation do you do for a picture? Do you plan it? Do you do sketches?

CF: It varies. Usually I fiddle with an idea. I do a few sketches to sort things out; then I get right into painting. Then, of course, I get right into repainting and repainting and repainting. The more preliminary work I do—the more sketches—the less likely the thing is ever going to end up being a picture. I waste huge amounts of time this way. It takes forever to recognize a fundamental mistake.

GH: What gets you started on a painting?

CF: There is no easy answer to that. All sorts of things get me started: something I've felt, someone or something I've seen, something I've read. Other paintings get me started.

GH: There is a lot of talk about your accessibility.

CF: At the risk of sounding simple-minded, I have no interest in being inaccessible. Too often obscurity is just a dodge. It has nothing to do with the complexity of the issue at hand. It's always safe to be incomprehensible. Who knows—someone with money or a column might think you're a genius.

8

It was during his first semester at Greenhurst that Freeze met Sarah Fenwick, a young photographer studying with Martin Kalinowski. She was working on her second major project—photographing famous artists standing in front of pictures they wish they had painted. She took a photo of Shield standing in front of Van Eyck's *Man in a Red Turban*. She and Freeze had coffee. Coffee led to racquetball, racquetball led to friendship, friendship led to affection, affection led to something more.

That summer there was a group show of Shield's students at the Skidmore Gallery. Freeze's entry, a small still life that he thought badly overworked, was singled out with one other picture as being the only successes.

In November Freeze and Sarah were married. They had flown down to San Diego to stay with friends near Windansea Beach in La Jolla—a place made semi-famous by Timothy Lamb, a Ph.D. sociologist turned fop journalist in an essay about lollygagging teenagers and surfing. A decade later Freeze would do a series of beach pictures that alluded to this time and place.

(EXCERPTS FROM THE UNPUBLISHED JOURNALS OF CHRISTOPHER FREEZE)

It always worries me when I find myself agreeing with Brian (we both hated the Hahn show last month), so I am relieved to find out that we are back to disagreeing—this time about Yates. He has a new show at the Melser Gallery and Brian was all over it with adjectives—playful, profound, serious, overwhelming. It didn't strike me as any of these things. A Yates picture is basically just a great big blob of modulated color. If you sit and stare at it long enough you will hypnotize yourself and you will see things. If you are Brian, you will think those things you are seeing are the mysterious metaphysical musings of a master. If you are me, you will think those things are the not-so-mysterious epiphenomena of a self-induced hallucination. You can probably find anything you want in one of Yates's pictures if you try hard enough. That doesn't mean it's there.

I'm sitting on a bench at Mill Pond watching the ducks and geese paddle about in the cocoa-colored water. They were interested in me when I first sat down—when they thought I was going to feed them—but they are not interested in me now. They turn their backs, cluck, shake their ducky-butts, and paddle off without any pretense of regard, and I am left here alone to think about the painting—the one waiting stupidly in my studio. Waiting for me to do what—come back and try again? It's a mess. It's all over

41

the place. What is the point of trying again? Why should I think this time will be *the* time—the time I finally figure it out, the time I make a little progress. What distinguishes this time from the hundred times that preceded it? Dr. Hatcher says I should keep perspective (who doesn't love a good art pun?), that I shouldn't worry about feeling the way I do about this picture because I always feel this way to one degree or another about every picture I'm working on, and in the end I am always wrong; that unfortunately for me, my process (such as it is) seems to require prolonged periods of hopelessness. Just because I've been wrong about pictures in the past doesn't mean I'm wrong about this one; maybe this time is *the* time—the time I'm right and there is no end to this gloom and desolation. But even if I am wrong again and I do get through this picture, there has to be something not right about a person who works this way, something that is or isn't fixable. If it is fixable, Hatcher needs to be getting on with it. If it isn't, then what is the point of our continuing to meet? It makes him a little richer and maybe I feel momentarily a bit better, but I can't imagine any reasonable cost/benefit analysis that would suggest it was really worth it.

Michelle is obsessed with the Kennedy family—especially with JFK. She seems to know most of what there is to know about him—the date he was born (May 29, 1917), what schools he went to (Dexter, Riverdale, Choate), what president he was (35th).

She wishes almost more than anything that she had had a chance to meet him. "I know just the dress I would have worn," she says.

❖

Shield and I sit at opposite ends of the spectrum: I need peace and quiet to prosper; he needs drama and hubbub.

❖

Very cold night. If only they made gloves for your feet.

❖

Julie Frye, a friend of Sarah's from way back, flew in last night from New York. She took the red-eye to save a little money. She arrived tired and jet-lagged and not at all ready to find out the airline had lost her luggage. She wanted to take it in stride like a well-traveled grownup, but she couldn't. Apparently it's one thing to suddenly have no underwear, but something else entirely when you are phobic about bad breath to not have a toothbrush.

❖

The latest argument between Mark and Sophia seems to have revolved almost entirely around Sophia's career. She is an assistant to the Executive Director of the Creative Advocacy Network, a nonprofit organization set up to focus on fundraising for the arts. Mark wants her to look for something else—something in the fundraising for childhood diseases area perhaps. Right now he is working for his father's insurance company, but his plan is to become a politician, to run for the State Senate, and he is worried that working for CAN Sophia is bound to end up involved in the financing of some egregiously reprehensible project, something constitutionally protected but nonetheless repugnant to most sentient beings—and, in particular, repugnant to this or that group of sentient beings whose support Mark is going to need if he is ever going to get to be what he wants to be.

The first thing I noticed about Barnes was the kelpish pile of curly brown hair. The second thing was the dramatic chinlessness. He told me how nice it was to finally meet me and thanked me for agreeing to do the interview. He said he has been wanting to do something on me for a while, that he knew David Ford, and that David Ford would vouch for him. He seemed genuinely perplexed by my desire to be left alone—unprofiled, unmonographed. He couldn't imagine not wanting to be written about. (Perhaps I should start looking into him, become the profiler of my profiler.) He says he just finished a paper on a subject he knows is near and dear to my heart—the death of the art critic. He will send me a copy. He has a distinctly off-putting way. It is—I'm relieved to say—unhideable. There is no chance of being charmed by him, of being lulled into trusting him, so there should be no chance of ever being confused about his real intentions.

He puts way too much sugar in his coffee.

(EXCERPTS FROM VARIOUS REVIEWS)

"In Freeze one finds a highly distilled experience hiding behind a purposefully haphazard-seeming brushwork. If De Kooning had decided to deface a Matisse the results, I suspect, would have looked something like this."

9

It was in early February that Freeze was introduced to Charles Safadi, the man who would become his first and only dealer. Safadi, bored and unhappy with his life as an accountant, had recently abandoned his wife and job to start a gallery. A slight, nervous, mumbling man, he developed a reputation for spotting talent almost immediately. Erick Falco, an expressionist landscape painter who was one of Safadi's early discoveries, had just signed with a predatory competitor leaving a hole in Safadi's gallery schedule. He offered the slot to Freeze, and Freeze accepted.

Closed up in a small studio he had found in Portland's dilapidated (but soon to be gentrified) warehouse district, Freeze started to paint. He reworked a couple of old canvases, things from his thesis show, and moved rapidly on to other subjects. The pace was not one he found congenial. The pieces he produced were uneven and did not fit together in the way he would have liked. There were passages here and there that seemed repetitious, others that seemed underdone, and still others that seemed simply sloppy. Freeze would never be able to decide exactly how he felt about this debut—sometimes he made allowances and gave himself a pass, but mostly he was disappointed. There were elements one would find later in his more mature work—a thoroughly promiscuous use of paint, for example—but Freeze felt the show on the whole had been marred by the inclusion of too much juvenilia.

(EXCERPTS FROM THE UNPUBLISHED JOURNALS OF CHRISTOPHER FREEZE)

Ran into David Hoff today. I haven't seen him in several months and to tell you the truth I wouldn't mind not seeing him for several more. There is nothing especially wrong with David, but there is nothing especially right with him either, and being in this mood it seems I need that little something extra to fire up my pathetically unfired socializing instinct. We had a chat in part about his upcoming optometrist's appointment but mostly about nothing. He wanted to know if I was interested in grabbing a bite to eat. I wasn't really, but because I've ducked him so many times lately I didn't feel like I could do it again, so I said sure. He wanted to go to the Everett Street Bistro. I like the place, but we have a complicated history that involves teeming crowds and lengthy waits to be seated. David said he was a regular and since it was a Tuesday and we were near the end of the lunch hour, there shouldn't be any problem. He was right. We were able to make the transition from men-on-the-street to customers with little of the usual confusion. I had the French toast because I almost always have breakfast food if I can and the version ESB does is exceptional—a two-inch thick plank of bread soaked in Grand Marnier custard and served with real maple syrup. I love the color. In one of the pictures I did of Sarah I used it for her hair. It took a while to get right, but hair the color of this French toast—it was lovely.

❖

Things have been getting worse for a while. I have tried to ignore it, but I'm not sure I can anymore. It started with these small irregularities—these peculiar responses to things. Now these responses are bigger, more peculiar, more frequent. I haven't mentioned this to Sarah because I don't want her getting worried, but I think maybe she is worried already.

❖

Monica dropped by this morning for a cup of coffee and to complain about her horrible children: Jeffrey, age fifteen, and Jennifer, age thirteen. She has been doing this a lot lately—dropping by to complain—not because it really helps (what could help), but because apparently she sort of has to. She wishes she liked her kids more than she does, but she can't, not really. It's easy to understand. I mean, just look at them. Listen to them. She has a point. These are not your typical teenage terrors. They have a special sort of awfulness about them that goes way beyond the usual "troubled adolescent" stuff. Hostile, sarcastic, rude—Jeffrey is pretty obviously a sociopath, and sullen, eye-shadow-abusing Jennifer is nothing if not mean-hearted. Monica knows what they say about parents and what parents are responsible for, but she can't believe she and Alex—as difficult to live with as they are—could be wholly to blame for these two. Other, more malignant forces must have been at work.

❖

Michelle isn't looking too good today. She is tired and has a lump on her head. She got spooked last night. She was in bed half asleep when she heard something in the hallway outside her apartment—something that wasn't right—some sort of clawing or scraping sound that stopped and started as it drew closer. She tried for a time to think reasonably about what this could possibly be, but it didn't sound like anything she had ever heard before—it sounded angry, metallic, evil— and she couldn't help but wonder if maybe it had something to do with Liz and her recent dabblings in the occult (Liz was bored, between boyfriends, and the aquarium just wasn't enough); maybe something had gone wrong, but more likely she thought (because she didn't really believe in the occult) it was one of those rapists or murderers who are always being acci- dentally released from maximum security, so she got the baseball bat out from under her bed and slipped into Liz's room to wake her up, which wasn't as easy a thing to do as you might think because Liz sleeps like a dead person and Michelle had to whisper so whoever (or whatever) it was out there wouldn't hear her; know she was on to him (or it); know she was a she and right there, nubile and terrified, on the other side of that cheap apartment door. Wake up, wake up, wake up, Michelle said softly, but of course sleeping-like-a-dead-person Liz didn't, so Michelle had to give her a little shake, which proved to be a mistake. It worked in that it woke Liz up, but it woke her up suddenly and big—she had no idea what was going on, she didn't know it was Michelle there in her room, she just saw someone—one of those rapists or murderers who are always being accidentally released from maximum security—standing over her with a baseball bat so she screamed and kicked out, sending the totally-unprepared-for-this Michelle flying across the room headfirst into an ugly mahogany dresser.

One of the most interesting things to me about Hannah is her attitude toward men. She thinks very few of them like women. Kevin and I are approved as exceptions.

I could tell what was in store for me after that first interview with Barnes, but for Sarah's sake I've agreed to do a second. She thinks I am being just a little too wary. If this second interview confirms my suspicions about what he is up to, then that is it; I won't be doing any more.

50

(EXCERPTS FROM VARIOUS REVIEWS)

"A large part of the argument about Freeze centers on the distortion one finds in his work. There is one side that says he relies too heavily on it, that he sacrifices too much of representation's power, and another side that says the work is not distorted enough, that a slavish attachment to the identifiable object restricts the freedom of expression that is at the heart of the best contemporary work. It is said as if nothing true lay between these two positions."

10

The Freezes moved into a nondescript little house on Lincoln Street that they rented from a grocery-store clerk and her postal-worker husband. They bought a clownish Dalmatian they named Wally—a goofy, loving dog who cheered an uncheerful Freeze right up. Unfortunately, over the previous few months Freeze had gotten himself into a place where, Dalmatian or not, he couldn't stay sunny for long. His days in the studio were tormenting him. There was what he wanted to do and what he could do—and no way, it seemed, of bridging the divide. Sarah worked for a bank and took pictures on the weekends while Christopher did tutorial work to help make ends meet. One day without any special warning, Freeze hit a psychic wall. He simply could not or would not get out of bed. He stayed there and stayed there and stayed there. Sarah called an ambulance.

(EXCERPTS FROM THE UNPUBLISHED JOURNALS OF CHRISTOPHER FREEZE)

Another call from Erik so, against my better judgment, I went over. When I got there I found his girlfriend Kathy. She had just dropped in. I don't really care for her very much. I should probably try to figure out why. For one thing, there is the ostentatiousness of her hairdo—a great huge pile of stuff going every which way. But mostly I think it's the politics. She is a Republican. I'm not crazy about them in general, but I have an easier time making allowances for the male of the species. The thing she has going in her favor is that she doesn't talk politics—not like Sarah who is indefatigable.

When I walked in Kathy and Erik were sitting on the couch. K looked up and said Hi—we're looking at knees. Erick is thinking about getting a double replacement. They had a dozen brochures spread out on the coffee table, each promoting its own brand of new technology.

Kathy was fascinated by the fact that some replacement knees were now ceramic. Apparently somewhere in her younger, less orthodox days, she had been interested in ceramics and had gone to evening classes at a hobby shop. She specialized in flower vases. Everyone in her family has four or five masterpieces. She wanted to know if I had ever given any thought to working in the medium. I said no—never. Then, of course, she brought up Picasso.

He worked in ceramics some, you know.

But he didn't do knees.

No, he didn't do knees.

Funny when I think about it—and sad—how almost every extended conversation I have ever had with a non-artist contains a reference to Picasso. I can't decide how I feel about it. Is it a triumph of art or a triumph of marketing? Is there a difference anymore?

❖

Back over to Erick's. He was alone except for his anomalous cat, Clarence. I always forget he has it. It's just the wrong sort of cat for him—a Siamese. He is not the sort of person who should have this sort of cat—or any cat at all for that matter. The fact that he does have it suggests there is a secret side to him—which seems unlikely because he is one of those forthright types who doesn't seem complicated enough to have sides at all, let alone secret ones. He said he had just gotten off the telephone with his nephew. This seems to always be the case with Erick—that he is just getting off the phone with some relative. He has a huge, intricately organized extended family. I've paid enough attention to know the names of his brothers and sisters, but I draw the line at nieces, nephews, and cousins (once or twice removed). He had been talking to this nephew about investing in real estate. Erick is against it at this time. If you're going to be putting money into something right now, apparently it should be something that is government-backed.

❖

Sarah and Monica are planning another photo project together—the subject this time: ambiguous architectural detail; i.e., things that remind you of other things.

She is a strange bird, Monica. Next to Sarah, I think her closest relationship is with her psychologist.

❖

Brian's subject du jour was Geoffrey Wyatt, the owner of the Wyatt Gallery in Seattle, and the role he has been playing in the local art world. He is in the middle of staging another one of his groundbreaking extravaganzas (Evolution or Revolution) focusing on a new group of artists doing the sort of thing he likes to see being done—simple, overdramatized stuff that always seems to get a lot of attention. Brian—not surprisingly—has mixed feelings. He doesn't much care for the art in the show—which he says is derivative and non-serious—but he likes the fact that the show has everybody talking.

Again, I can't help feeling Brian's real problem here is not with the work (it's the sort of thing he often goes in for), but with its success.

❖

"Harmless" is another of Brian's favorite damning adjectives.

❖

Lunch with Mark and Kevin at VC. Still nothing from Wicks vis-à-vis Kevin's portfolio, but unexpected news from Los Angeles: a better teaching job if he wants it, and he thinks he might. Mark's question: Has he talked to Hannah about it? Kevin's answer: Not yet.

❖

Where does the money come from—it is as big a mystery as where the inspiration comes from.

(EXCERPTS FROM VARIOUS REVIEWS)

" 'Distant Travels' is a large-scale group painting (there are eight figures—nine if you count the dog). It is strongly reminiscent of the old French salon-style painting, the sort of thing with which artists once sought to establish their careers and reputations. A complex interior space—with chairs, ladders, carpets, ships, slippers, lutes, and a classically reclining nude glowing at the center like some sort of iconic pilot light—it's a spirited picture wide open for interpretation. Read from left to right, from dark to light, it seems to be, among other things, a sort of contemplation of the infamous 'eternal feminine.'"

(EXCERPTS FROM VARIOUS INTERVIEWS)

BB: Was art school good for you?

CF: It was good to be around people who were interested in the same things I was interested in—but "good for me," I'm not sure. I think it was a little too nurturing. They said "yes" to everything. I think it might have been a little more helpful if they had occasionally said "no." All those yeses—they're fine in the formative years, but this was supposed to be the beginning of adulthood. You need something to bump up against. It's how you figure out for certain what you believe.

BB: You were a difficult student—rebellious?

CF: There was nothing to rebel against except rebelling—which I did for a while, but that got tiresome so I rebelled against rebelling against rebelling by becoming, once again, rebellious. In the end, of course, I just got bored.

11

In early April Freeze was invited to enter a piece in the annual group show at the Skidmore Gallery, the gallery that represented Ethan Shield. He sent a picture titled "Cup," a gooey still life of his beloved coffee mug—the mug Sarah had stolen for him from a café in Mission Hills.

It was about the time of this show that Freeze started work on a picture he called *Captured*, a work some argumentative academics have been so bold as to consider his first truly significant canvas. It is still a controversial piece today as it seems to sit on the cusp of a stylistic before and after. A handful of professional malcontents have dismissed it as an earlier, distinctly inferior version of the canvas they consider to be his first truly significant one: *Muses*. While it seems obvious that Freeze transferred certain effects, certain structures, *Captured*—a group of undifferentiated figures blindfolded and bound together into a sort of vegetal bunch by a tangle of leafy, kudzu-like vines— was a thing unto itself. In it you can see Freeze struggling against the sanctioned, senior-class seriousness that came so easily to him—a seriousness of which he was, at this point, only periodically suspicious.

(EXCERPTS FROM THE UNPUBLISHED JOURNALS OF CHRISTOPHER FREEZE)

Minimalism and the idea of flatness got mixed together and the result was stuff that was not very interesting to look at—but worse, not much fun to manufacture. To miss out on the fun of paint, the slopping it around, the brushwork—for me that would be deprivation. Look at Rubens, Van Gogh, DeKooning—part of the pleasure you get from them is the pleasure transferred by the painter who is indulging himself in the primordial love of mess-making.

❖

Bullshit is a preservative. There is nothing better for a reputation than a hopelessly convoluted analysis by one of the tenured gods of critical commentary.

❖

Safadi is grumbling again about the hapless Randalls—William and Helen. They just passed on one of Longworth's pieces—a still life of bottles and bricks. W is a dentist and H has a small catering business. They want to be thought of as collectors, but they are not really collecting all that much. They have to see everything and be talked to and talked to before they buy. But they haven't been buying—not lately. They can't really afford the best pictures so Safadi has to stick with showing them the moderate and lower-priced stuff, and the moderate and lower-priced stuff seems almost always to be a disappointment. It makes William—who in his heart of hearts just wants to get in on the ground floor of something—feel like he is being hustled, and Helen just gets mopier and mopier about it all.

❖

People are always trying to fix Michelle up with someone because of her personality and because she isn't seeing anyone in particular right now and she seems like someone who should be. Everyone who comes in the place and knows her seems to have a single friend or two roaming loose around the periphery of their social circle—friends who they are sure would be just right for her. I have single friends too—painters. Lots of them. Most are a little too old for Michelle, but those who aren't are still painters like the others and not right for her at all because— well, they're painters, and painters aren't right for anyone.

❖

Lots of hubbub around here about the show that isn't going to happen—the Hartung show at Linden's. It was scheduled to open May 1, but now we hear that something has gotten up his lordship's nose, and it has been cancelled. Hartung is probably Portland's most famous living crank—one of very few painters I know with an actual cult following. We haven't seen anything from him in fifteen years, and now it looks like we're going to have to wait another fifteen (or until he dies and the estate is exploited by his son Sebastian). It's probably just as well. A show would have ruined the rumors about what it was he had been up to. It would cut into the fun of scabrous speculation.

❖

Had lunch with David Ford, Colleen's ex. He's one of those low-blood-pressure guys who seems preternaturally lackadaisical about everything. I don't really know what happened between him and Colleen (I don' really think they know either), but whatever it was, it took a while. Colleen used to say that David was never fully there, but I think actually he was. She thought there was some essential part of him that he was keeping out of reach for some reason because something about David always seemed to suggest as much. But I don't think there ever was some obscured or unavailable something else. I think what seemed to be there was really all there was, and that, as it turns out, was just not enough.

❖

Maybe I'll just wander up to the Center. Besides the coffeeshop, there is a bakery, a real-estate office, a cleaners, a pizza place, and a hair salon that was about to go out of business but now isn't. They were offering cheap haircuts in an expensive-haircut neighborhood and it wasn't working—not until the recession hit. Now people are looking for ways to save money here and there, and things have picked up for them. They are the only business in the center that is doing better this year than last. Maybe I'll go up and look at it.

❖

It wasn't the worst that could have happened. When she talked to me I answered, and I seemed to be making sense.

❖

Hannah is not interested in moving to Los Angeles while Kevin is pretty certain he is going to have to. Trouble in the wind.

❖

Barnes is not going to go out of his way to make me look good. If he goes out of his way, it will be to make himself look good—fair, astute, generous. How I look will be immaterial. This is something I should keep in mind as I talk with him. It shouldn't be difficult.

(EXCERPTS FROM VARIOUS REVIEWS)

"One can overdo ruthlessness—like Lucian Freud,

for example—or they can use it judiciously to make a point. Freeze has chosen the latter strategy. One is never overwhelmed by the brutality of his observations—they are lured in and seduced."

12

Tense and unhappy with what he took to be the aimlessness of his work, Freeze started drinking again—heavily. He wanted to produce something reinvigorating, something he could use to convince himself that he was not just wasting his time. He hoped that something might be his *Sartre Suite*, a group of four stylized portraits of the recently deceased philosopher—one with sunglasses, one with a gag, one holding a handkerchief to his nose, one with his hands tied behind his back. Freeze had hoped they might prove ripe for variation (a nihilist's version of Monet's haystacks), but they did not. They remained an isolated group complete in and of themselves. Safadi was not encouraging. He liked two of the pictures, but he did not think they were especially sellable. Freeze agreed, but he kept on—not with the same subject, but in the same stylistic vein, which sought to emphasize simultaneously both the viscosity of paint and the viscosity of certain ideas.

(EXCERPTS FROM THE UNPUBLISHED JOURNALS OF CHRISTOPHER FREEZE)

Couldn't sleep so got up and headed to the studio.

Wally wanted some time off from guarding Sarah, so I let him tag along.

❖

I had breakfast at the Bijou with Safadi. It was his idea. I knew something was up because when he called to invite me there was a "something's up" in his voice, and when he arrived it was not in his usual early-morning breakfast clothes (khakis and sweat-shirt) but in his tastefully flamboyant Gallery Own-er's gear (black turtleneck, black slacks, black sports coat). X, of course, led us to our table. I don't know his name. He is the Bijou's version of a maitre d', and he has been there forever—a taller, handsomer, leaner version of the ill-fated monologist Spaulding Gray. He slithers through the aisles—between cus-tomers and servers—like a mongoose through a maze, leading us to our special place among the special people: the politicos, the culturati, the poseurs, the hash-hounds. Safadi has news. Apparently the Simon Baker Museum in Chicago is interested in naming me as the featured artist in their next "New and Note-worthy" exhibition. I am supposed to be excited. The Baker is important—it is the beginning of the begin-ning of so many reputations...the gateway to New York, if you will. But I am not excited. I know the Baker—it's very much a mainstream sort of place—and while I have nothing against it or the people they have chosen in the past for this honor, I don't think my stuff would fit in very well and I am not really interested in getting involved. My problem is not with the venue as much as it is with the surrounding hoopla. Selection as Mr. New-and-Noteworthy comes with obligations—obligations to attend functions, to attend parties, to give lectures, to be interviewed. I didn't want to let on how I felt about this—not right away—because it was obvious that Safadi had been working tirelessly behind the scenes to get it for me. I let him tell me more and then led him gently into a discussion of the hoopla issue, expressing a mild version of my not-so-mild aversion. He promised to discuss the exact nature of the commitment with the Baker Board, at which point I smiled and asked him to pass the blueberry syrup.

❖

Turmoil at the Turner house. It seems Alex, Monica's husband, has been having an affair with one of his students, a pretty pixie-type named Elizabeth Something-or-Other. The young lady had apparently found her professor's exquisite understanding of *Pride and Prejudice* to be knee-weakening. Alex is saying it meant nothing and that it is over—but, of course, that's not really the point, now is it?

❖

Patrick Hudson is supposed to come by and look at this new picture. I hope he cancels. He doesn't know anything about art, but he likes you to pretend he does. You're expected to nod a lot and look like you're taking him seriously. Why doesn't he visit

Jeff Stewart? Stewart goes in for this sort of thing—strangers in the studio. Why am I going crazy and not Jeff Stewart?

❖

I have a feeling Barnes is going to be hard on me. He will tell himself it is his job, but in truth I think it's more a matter of predisposition—a certain inherent maliciousness masquerading as moral integrity. Selling me down the river isn't really going to trouble him in the least. He may act conflicted, but that's really just for show.

❖

Every time I think about the Randalls and what it is they seem to be looking for, I think about those two Russians, Komar and Melamid, who did that satirical survey of artist preferences around the world. They asked people in a dozen different countries what sort of pictures they liked best—outdoor ones or indoor, traditional or modern, religious or nonreligious. They found the hands-down favorite thing cross-culturally was a landscape with trees and water. The dominant color, of course, was blue. I have the feeling that the Randalls are very much blue-landscape people who are trying not to be. They are trying to get away from this instinctive inclination of theirs—far enough away to seem out of the ordinary, but not so far away as to seem peculiar.

❖

Do I let this picture go? Will it come back a year from now to haunt me with its imperfections?

❖

Lunch with Mark and Kevin at VC. No final decisions from Kevin about the Los Angeles job, but unexpected news from Mark: He has been offered a Legislative Aide position in Sacramento. Kevin's question: Has he talked to Sophia about it? Mark's answer: Not yet.

❖

When I look at Obermeier's stuff I don't see someone trying to say something—I see someone trying to make a few bucks.

❖

It's almost impossible to trace my original feeling for Sarah from where we are now back to where we began. She was pretty, she was smart, she was funny, she took marvelous pictures with a less-than-marvelous camera, and she was a pleasure to be around. I don't remember thinking anything more than that about her until one evening we somehow ended up at Whozits, a bar near the school. It was a dark, not-too-clean place full of cigarette smoke and noise. We sat in a corner, had a few vodkas, and talked for an hour or two. It started then, I think—whatever it was that led to us becoming us.

(EXCERPTS FROM VARIOUS REVIEWS)

"Freeze seems to be painting for a small, aesthetically unaffiliated group of art-interested people—people who respect both the accessible and the arcane (but neither at the other's expense), people with little time for the self-regarding exclusivity of most contemporary weirdness."

13

It was in the fall that Freeze had his second breakdown. Everyone saw it coming. He was taken to see a psychologist, a Dr. Gabriel Hatcher, and diagnosed with depression. Freeze refused medication, but agreed to start seeing Hatcher regularly. He had hopes the doctor might be of some help, that they might to some degree understand one another because Hatcher was a painter himself—not what you would call a particularly serious one, but serious enough to be at least passingly familiar with the issues of the enterprise. Throughout the winter Freeze's mood improved.

(EXCERPTS FROM THE UNPUBLISHED JOURNALS OF CHRISTOPHER FREEZE)

My pictures are, in large part, the simple products of instinct. Any theory involved—well, that came later as I was always being asked to explain myself and I felt I had to come up with something.

How long will it take Monica to figure out what she thinks about this thing with Alex? Will she ever

70

really figure it out—or will she just get tired and for-give him (or just get tired and tell him to go).

Alex's best explanation so far seems to be that this is just something that sort of happened. (He thinks that something that just sort of happened—that is, something someone lets happen as opposed to some-thing someone makes happen—is a lesser sort of crime and qualifies for a lesser sort of punishment.) It is not an explanation that has won him much support.

❖

I am feeling tense. Matt Farino, the weatherman for Channel 8 News, is forecasting a heat wave. It's a few days off, but I can't help obsessing about it. I try to pay attention to other stories—like the one about exercising your pets so they don't get paunches and arthritis—but I can't. These forecasters are wrong all the time about snow, but they're almost never wrong about the heat.

Also, I am tired of waiting for word from Safadi about the sale of *Richard's Requiem*, which has been sitting in Anthony Lochner's lap for a couple of weeks now. Buy it, don't buy it—he needs to make up his mind. This waiting, this not knowing—it's making me sick to my stomach.

❖

Talked with Safadi. He told me not to worry. He said Lochner's taking a long time to decide was a good thing. I told him I didn't know if it was a good thing, but it seemed a typical thing for people like Lochner—people with their prerogatives and their lives of privilege. What does Sarah say? She says to be quiet and to wait.

❖

Still nothing from Safadi about Lochner. Sarah suggested I try to focus my attention on something else—like the upcoming City Council election, but it isn't really much of a race and I don't like the guy who is so obviously going to win (he is a long-time aide to the outgoing Councilman). He says he wants to represent everyone, not just a small coterie of like-minded ideologues, but he doesn't have a sincere bone in his body. He simply oozes calculation. He never misses a chance to step in front of a microphone or a camera. He'll probably be fine, but I can't get enthu-siastic enough to be distracted.

❖

Michelle and Liz have started taking classes in spiritualism. The woman who teaches the class is sublimely confident. She seems to believe what she is saying, which makes it easier for both Michelle and Liz to believe—part of it, anyway. On Wednesday nights now—from eight to nine—they gather with fellow travelers to explore a friendly, jasmine-scented world of answers and awe.

❖

Colleen called me about Safadi. She thinks he may be cracking up. Apparently he got into some sort of physical confrontation with Hoagland last night at a meeting of the Art Dealers Association. The meeting was at Drumlin's Gallery, and in the scuffle (which was mostly just a lot of awkward, middle-aged pushing and shoving) a Bennett Barryhill piece got broken. (Barryhill is a mathematician turned glass sculptor.) The Association is trying to handle the incident internally, but there is always a chance—especially with Hoagland involved—that it could go legal, which would be devastating for Safadi as he already has some pretty serious money troubles.

Colleen thinks Safadi needs some attention, that he is emotionally and financially adrift, that he needs some looking after. She would do it herself, but she can't right now because she has her hands full looking after a new husband—so she wants one of his artists to do it, but not just anyone. It has to be the right one, and most (me included, she says) are not capable of looking after themselves let alone anyone else. She thinks he might be developing a twitch.

Colleen wants me to drop whatever it is I'm doing right now and join Safadi on a little Arts Association junket. It seems the RAA is putting together one of those traveling symposia: The Painter, The Gallery, and The Contemporary Scene. A panel of painters, gallery owners, and journalists are being asked to spout-off at the art museum in Eugene one night and then the next night at the art museum in North Bend. Reluctantly I have agreed.

❖

Safadi has been pretty blunt with the Randalls about being a salesman. He has made it as clear to them as he can that selling paintings is the way he makes his living—that his job, as he sees it, is simply to show them the sort of things they have, at one time or another, said they wanted to see. He only talks to them about the stuff he believes in, stuff he thinks it is possible they would like. It's up to them to decide if they want it. He has never presented anything to them as an "investment." So far he has shown them more than four hundred pictures. They have bought fourteen. It has been almost a year since their last purchase.

❖

Sophia is not interested in moving to Sacramento while Mark is pretty certain he is going to have to. Trouble in the wind.

❖

Barnes is working on his interview technique. He wants to seem loosey-goosey to get me off guard. Only occasionally do we sit down with a list of prepared questions.

74

❖

I have consented to the interviews, but I am under no illusions. Barnes will try to seem friendly (not easy for him) and sympathetic, to be on my side. But he will not be on my side—he will be on his own side. It will be convenient for him to assume that I am not telling him the whole story. He will use the elusiveness of truth as an excuse to imply untruths that have the virtue, at least, of being tantalizing.

(EXCERPTS FROM VARIOUS REVIEWS)

"There are places in some of these paintings where Freeze gets carried away with the expressive stroke—particularly in some of the earlier pieces. You can see him struggling to get this inclination under control. Over time he has grown consistently more confident and subtle in his assertions."

14

In the spring Freeze began a group of sketches for a painting that would eventually become *Four Dead*. He continued to see Dr. Hatcher. They talked about Christopher's new mustache and the recent death of Tennessee Williams (Freeze having been much affected by *The Glass Menagerie* when he first read it).

(EXCERPTS FROM THE UNPUBLISHED JOURNALS OF CHRISTOPHER FREEZE)

On the surface Monica continues to be Monica. She has her headaches, her insomnia, her six flossings a day, her complicated dietary concerns. Deeper down, though, there seems to be a new seriousness to her insanity.

I can't do anything this morning. Inspiration, hope, know-how—all missing. Lost like my car keys. There is never a good time to feel like this, but this is probably the least good time imaginable as I've been on the edge of the edge for way too long now.

❖

Safadi showed the Randalls a new picture the other day—one of Kruger's enigmatic portraits, a piece he thought would be just right, a substantive thing that was in their price range—the sort of picture he hoped would get them buying, get them feeling once again like they were in the game, on the hunt, part of it. But it wasn't. They declined the thing after about a three-minute look-see saying it was simply too bleak.

❖

Just got into Eugene. I don't know who booked the motel, but the place is a nightmare—singeing smell of disinfectant, water-stained ceilings, cacophony of clashing patterns (floral rug, geometric bedspread, scotch-plaid armchair)—the sort of place where firing up the hairdryer makes lights in the place flicker and dim.

The drive down was a nightmare, too. I didn't know this about Safadi, but apparently he is one of those people who has to look at you when he talks. I would prefer he looked at the road.

❖

When it comes to barista work Michelle is not what you would call a natural. She hates steaming milk (it curls her hair), she can't tell an excellent espresso extraction from a mediocre one, and she has a bad attitude toward iced drinks in general. She went

77

through an intensive four-day training program when she started, but nothing much came of it. She never bonded with the ethos. She found the machinery to be intimidating and industrial.

❖

Preoccupied with arithmetic. One small drawing equals how many hot showers?

❖

Brian droning on with more than his usual chic incoherence—this time about conceptual art. It's numbing, blank, not to be taken seriously or thought about for any length of time, etc., etc. But, of course, no sooner has this crime against coolness escaped his mouth than he's looking for linguistical cover. He starts talking in tongues about a whiff of the zeitgeist, about the virtues of contemporaneity, about itching a need for the now. It's not for the ages, this stuff—for the ages is for chumps, people with mortgages, people with plans for the future, people with three-car garages, people with premium cable service. Conclusion: classic Brian—gobbledygook on a cracker.

❖

Sarah is easily spooked. Her startled reaction to unstartling things invariably startles me and sets off some sort of primordial swearing response.

❖

Leafing through *The New Yorker* this afternoon I noticed—for the I-don't-know-how-many-eth time—a small ad in the back of the magazine for "European Berets." I noticed it because it was placed there by our very own John Helmer. It's a small thing—1 by 2 ½ inches—with a postage-sized photo of a young, slightly smiling, black-turtlenecked Mr. Helmer wearing one of these berets and pointing off casually into the unfathomable distance.

A local haberdasher, Mr. Helmer has been in business here since 1921. I've run into him on the street. The newspaper did a story on him when he turned eighty. (It was mostly about his exercise routine). What is he doing selling European berets in *The New Yorker*? There can't be much money in it. In my whole life I've known only one person who ever wore a beret: Adrian Renton. He was mentally ill.

It never fails—when someone is looking at a group of my pictures, they will always ask me if I have a favorite. I'll hesitate and try to act like I'm thinking about it, but I'm not. I've been asked too many times before. When I answer, I do it with the usual illustrative cliché—asking the asker if he or she has a favorite child. In truth, the answer to both of these questions is probably "yes," but, of course, it's not supposed to be. It is possible this answer is something you might be willing to admit to yourself, but it doesn't seem likely that it is the sort of thing you would be eager to admit to others.

❖

Had Kevin and Hannah over for dinner last night. It went better than we expected. It seems for the time being they have decided to pretend things between them are pretty much as they have always been.

❖

Barnes does not fully appreciate the relationship I have to my own past. I am not a retrospective sort. Huge chunks of my early life are unavailable to me. What there is is simple and so nowhere near wholly true.

(EXCERPTS FROM VARIOUS REVIEWS)

"When I stumbled on Christopher Freeze's picture *Nana* I was captured in spite of myself. I am not as a rule one of those people who can honestly say they are all that interested in sweet little old ladies. But there she was, seated quietly, alone, as sweet as she could be, and, well—interesting. Thatched with a cap of tight gray curls, her hands folded primly in her lap, she was a picture of propriety and patience. Her name (as I immediately imagined it) was Dorothy. I would not have wanted to be stuck behind her in the checkout line at the grocery store.

As I studied Dorothy I was bombarded by associations. Something about the pose—the erectness of the posture, the squared shoulders—reminded me of Giacometti; the isolation reminded me of Hopper;

the face reminded me of Rembrandt; the center of the scene reminded me (very distantly) of Bacon's caged Pope. None of these associations really had anything to do with the picture, however. The picture was pretty straightforwardly itself. Of course, that was— pretty straightforwardly—Freeze's point."

15

For a while Freeze didn't think he would be able to finish *Four Dead*, but something broke loose after a visit to Bandon where he had occupied himself for a week painting kite flyers. The image he was looking for found its way—a sort of cross between Goya's execution scene and Picasso's chaotic *Guernica* with lots of paint thrown in. The subject was Freeze's first historical one: the shooting of students at Kent State University by the Ohio National Guard. It was an unusual choice.

(EXCERPTS FROM THE UNPUBLISHED JOURNALS OF CHRISTOPHER FREEZE)

Sarah is picking Monica up at the train station. She has been in Seattle for a couple of days with her second-best friend, a veterinarian named Wendy Miller. Monica uses the train because she is afraid to drive. (She is not very good at being driven either— she always thinks you are going too fast or that you are too close or that someone—even though they don't have a signal on—is going to turn in front of you.) Mostly Monica takes the bus if she can, but she has been getting more and more concerned lately about contagious diseases—especially the sort of contagious diseases you get exposed to on public transportation. She is worried that she is on her way to becoming a full-fledged phobic.

❖

This morning's headache is a Category Five. I am working on a guest commentary for *Moment*, the local art mag. It looks like it's going to be an argument in favor of beauty. It's blasphemous. What I'm trying to say is that art doesn't have to be diverting, but it can be if it wants to—and at no cost to its truthfulness— that we in the arts community should think about being a little more ecumenical in our biases. It's not an easy argument to disguise. I've sprinkled it liberally with escape-clause qualifiers, but still I feel exposed.

❖

The panel talk went well. We had a decent crowd. They were attentive, they asked questions, they seemed to enjoy themselves. Most of my comments focused on Michael Rhodes, the hot new would-be arbiter of contemporary taste who has been getting a lot of attention lately—a complainer who I used to have some sympathy for, but who I have gotten tired of and worried about. I've agreed with him in the past about the triteness of contemporary political painting, but his recent boorish lambasting of "difficulty" has made me nervous and eager to disassociate myself. True, most of the "difficult" stuff he is complaining about isn't really "difficult," it's "desperately obscure"—trying to hide a lack of one thing or another (a lack of ideas, a lack of talent, a lack of imagination, a lack of competence)—but some of it is, and legitimately so. When these kind of complaints (not entirely misguided ones) pick up a certain sort of herd-momentum and get virulently anti-intellectual and have people like Rhodes going on and on like some sort of manifesto-mongering Monsignor, then I start to get worried about the baby being tossed out with the bathwater, the good going with the garbage. Some things can't be made appealing—not in the way Rhodes and his pals would like—but as long as they are made comprehensible I'm not only happy, I'm thankful.

Safadi spent his time talking about the competition between galleries—what it was and wasn't doing for the market, what the market was and wasn't doing for the artist, and what the artist was and wasn't doing for the gallery owner.

Jeff Barker, who writes for *The Riverview*, presented us with a list of his rules for reviewing. There were six or seven, I think, but I can only remember three: don't blame the painter you are reviewing for not being the painter you wish you were reviewing, include a graphic if you can—at least a thumbnail, and go easy on the flights of metaphorical fancy. Extended analogies may be fun and they may be an easy way to fill space, but more often than not they simply end up doing grievous harm to your credibility.

❖

It would be nice if Sarah had someone to talk to about me. It can't be easy—so many things she needs to say but can't (probably not even to herself).

❖

Bill Randall is getting frustrated and he is taking it out on Safadi. He is frowning a lot and making comments that suggest he feels he is somehow being double-dealt. He doesn't really seem to have any specific grievance—just a free-floating sense that something is going on at his expense.

❖

I am thankful for many things, but right up there near the top of the list is not knowing anyone who would think of dropping by without calling first.

❖

Kevin has been offered a promotion at Greenhurst. It's a better job than he had, but still not quite as good as the Los Angeles thing.

❖

Barnes and I are going to have very different ideas about what is and is not important. The Simon Baker debacle, for example. He will want to make something out of that I am sure.

(EXCERPTS FROM VARIOUS REVIEWS)

"Distracted by the energy that typifies his work, it is easy to overlook the complex heretical arguments being made in favor of good old-fashioned textbook expertise."

(EXCERPTS FROM VARIOUS INTERVIEWS)

DN: Are you always painting?

CF: Yes. I'm constant, but I'm slow. I'm slow because I find it hard. I've never cared anything about being faster, but I have always wished it were easier. It would make me feel more like I knew what I was doing.

DN: You haven't painted a lot. Is that because you paint slowly?

CF: In part. But mostly it's because I throw everything away. Or I used to. I throw less away now.

DN: Why is that?

CF: I suppose it's because I have finally realized that I am never going to be able to paint the way I want to (which would be considerably better than the way I do), but only the way I can. As I resign myself to this, I am able to keep more things.

DN: What about your success?

CF: What about it? It was never something I really cared about. I just wanted to get the picture right—or as right as I could. The success, such as it is, makes me nervous. I am still surprised when someone likes what I am doing.

16

After a number of reasonably discreet rejections, Safadi showed *Four Dead* to Martin Doyle, one of his oldest and flushest customers. Doyle was interested, but he wondered if a change or two could be made. Freeze declined. It was not a collaborative effort, he explained.

(EXCERPTS FROM THE UNPUBLISHED JOURNALS OF CHRISTOPHER FREEZE)

Today's drive was only a little less nightmarish than yesterday's. We were not going as fast, but the road was twistier.

❖

Safadi has been muttering about his feelings of isolation. He must be desperate. I told him what he needed was a good imaginary friend. They make no demands, they understand you, they are not repulsed by you, they always think you're right.

❖

I thought the motel in Eugene was a dump, but this place makes that one look opulent. This place, The Catwalk, is located a whole seventy-five yards off Highway 101. (Nothing rocks you to sleep like a downshifting eighteen-wheeler.) There was a note on the dresser warning me that I could be fined $100 for smoking out the bathroom window, that I would be held responsible for any undue destruction, and that an inventory was taken daily on the contents of the room.

❖

I don't think I have ever hurt Sarah's feelings on purpose. When I have hurt them, it has been by accident—and although I am always concerned, my estimate of the harm done is almost always less than her own.

❖

Can a piece of canvas get any blanker than this? The answer, of course, is no. At first I thought I was just having my usual trouble getting started, but this is day three and I'm still sitting here. It's beginning to feel like something else, something different, something more than my usual trouble getting started. There doesn't seem to be anything I can do to make it stop, to make this feeling go away. I'm exhausted. I've used up whatever I had to use up. Whatever I can do, I've done. I've tried it this way and that way until there are no more ways left. I could talk to Sarah, but she has had to listen to so much from me already.

❖

Michelle got her hair cut short and is asking everyone who comes in what they think about it. I haven't said much because I don't like it and I don't want to pretend I do. She has nice features for sure, but they are not nice enough for a haircut like this— for a haircut like this you need to be magazine-pretty and have a head the size of an orange.

❖

I'm always making notes to myself about pictures I want to paint. I'll be sitting in the living room leafing through a magazine or watching television and suddenly from out of who-knows-where I'll get an idea—or something that feels like an idea or something that feels like something that could lead to an idea if it was given a chance—and I'll write it down. Sometimes when I'm scribbling one of these notes Sarah will interrupt with something she is thinking or reading or with something that has come in the mail, and I'll say just a minute, I'm trying to write something down, but it will be too late because by the time I get back to it—one or two milliseconds later—it will be gone. Whatever it was, it will have depended on some sort of specific wording that was just being sensed—and with that specific wording gone, so too will everything else be, which, of course, is aggravating because even though I know it was probably nothing (something I would look at tomorrow and throw away), it could have been something because it has been something in the past—not often, but once or twice—and this could have been one of those times, but now I'll never know.

❖

I may feel a little down today, but there are things I can do and things I can think that I wouldn't be able to do or think if I headed off in the direction Dr. Hatcher is suggesting.

❖

Obligatory Art Museum shindig last night. As always, I hunted down Colleen's little gaggle. She and her friends are gifted and tireless talkers. I can join in without actually having to join in.

Nicholson was in attendance, of course. He was in a group that included Jay Shattuck, so I suspect he was stuck in the middle of a debate about nuclear power. I find Shattuck interesting, but I know he's not Nicholson's cup of tea. Sure enough, no sooner do I make this observation to myself than I see N slip smoothly away, champagne glass in hand, to another more promising group—the one he probably had his eye on from the beginning because it included, among other things, a distinctly unattached-looking woman in a distinctly tight blue dress. This is really what Jeffrey is in the business for—not the art, but the skinny women in blue dresses who circle its soirees.

He would be easy to hate if he wasn't so funny.

❖

Sarah had lunch with Sophia. She has started to put some distance between herself and Mark.

❖

Barnes's analysis of my life and its meaning will differ greatly from my own. It will be infinitely simpler. He will pad his pages with things that mattered to X, Y, and Z, but not really to me. What could he possibly know about the private things that sustained me?

(EXCERPTS FROM VARIOUS REVIEWS)

"'Duo' is a gutsy and arresting piece done in dramatic black and white—a beefed-up drawing carrying an extra expressive charge."

17

Taking advice from both his wife and his doctor, Freeze began a conscious struggle against his deeply-seated inclination to withdraw. He made a significant effort to reconnect with his old professor, Ethan Shield. He did a small picture for a group show that Shield was putting together and went to a few of Shield's regular gatherings allowing himself to get caught up a bit in the crowd—going out to dinner with John Dortman and for drinks on several occasions with Scott Hindricks.

(EXCERPTS FROM THE UNPUBLISHED JOURNALS OF CHRISTOPHER FREEZE)

I'm content to be an easel painter. Safadi once told me that if my pictures were bigger my reputation would be too. How much of one's work should be done in service to a reputation? I know it's naive to think as little as possible, but there you go.

❖

All nerves and no energy.

93

❖

No doubt this picture is a mistake, an imprudence, but the differentiating essence of the mistake is noteworthy, I think—or at least I hope it is.

❖

There are some lovely theories supporting abstract art—theories claiming an instinctual, pre-verbal sort of communication, theories equating abstract art to music in its untranslatable appeal. But for me—not just as an artist, but as a person who looks at pictures— a painting without a subject will always be a lesser painting. It might be famous and revered because of its place in what we call history or because someone with too much money has paid an astronomical price for it, but it is still lesser. However much I might like this or that abstract work, I will never be able to like it as much as I would a similarly wonderful semi-abstract one. The strength of my response to a subjective reality that is wholly imagined will never be as great as the strength of my response to a reality containing the minutest bit of objective meaning. Unfortunately I cannot admit this in public—not without being labeled a reactionary coot.

❖

Monica was over last night hiding out from her oppressive children. She and Sarah stayed up late watching *Dr. Zhivago* and weeping.

❖

Colleen thinks Safadi has been addled by grief, that he has recently lost the person closest to him (that person being the one he might have been if he had just done things a little differently). She thinks it might do him good to see someone: "What about Dr. Hatcher?" How do I answer that? I think Hatcher is probably fine for me, but for Safadi? I think Safadi should probably try to find someone a little more pharmaceutically oriented.

❖

Richard Butler has made it, but making it for him is different than making it for me. Making it for Rick means he is now considered a regular at Arnold's, a bar full of regulars—and not just any sort of regulars, but colorful ones with colorful nicknames—like the destitute trumpet player called Lips, the paraplegic homosexual called Wheelie, and the toothless narcoleptic known as Gumdrop. Rick's nickname, predictably enough, is Goat. It alludes to that mangy Mephistophelian goatee he has chosen as his signature. A dingy, low-lit place filled with the unwashed, the uncommitted, and the unemployed, Arnold's is one of those existential hog-wallows that prides itself on a dubious set of bona fides. A sort of retro stage set, it paraphrases another place and time—a place and time we readily assume to be realer, more substantive than the one we now inhabit.

95

❖

Safadi had an appointment to show the Randalls a new Mark Anderson picture yesterday, but only Helen showed up. She took a quick look and asked Safadi to call her bullheaded husband and badger him into coming down—which Safadi did.

They spent about half an hour with the picture *Haze Harbor* (a pair of tankers docked in dense fog), Safadi telling them what he could about its origins (one in a series of new marine paintings) and about the artist (bearded, corgi-owning, ex-art-history professor with a multiple personality disorder). After another half-hour of debating whatever it is they debate with each other, the Randalls made a decision: to delay a decision, to think about it. Not much maybe, but a radical enough departure from their recent usual as to seem like something.

❖

Lunch with Mark and Kevin at VC. Spent a lot of time talking about Wicks. Kevin finally got his rejection letter. The gallery thanked him for considering them and apologized for taking so long. They had a huge backlog of portfolios and had been exceedingly busy working on their fall show. His work, they said, did not fit their needs at this time, and they wished him the best of luck in placing it elsewhere. The big news from Mark: he is declining the Sacramento job.

❖

Barnes is interested in facts and incidents, and I am interested in the way my memory works. I am interested in what seemed important to me. He is interested in what might be interesting to a stranger with X number of dollars in his pocket. He is under pressure to be entertaining. Also, of course, he is supposed to be fair, objective, and responsible. When those things are in conflict he will invariably defer to the requirements of entertainment. It is assumed I know this and have come to terms with it.

(EXCERPTS FROM VARIOUS REVIEWS)

"Freeze can be just flat-out inscrutable. For example, there is his series of quasi-triptychs titled respectively *Diagnoses 1-3, Diagnoses 4-6,* and *Diagnoses 7-9.* Viewers may be encouraged to knit together their own little narrative, but these allegorical assemblages of personal travail steadfastly refuse both rational and linear explications. One can settle, perhaps, on a basic message about the hopeless complexity of human relationships, but messages are not the prize in Freeze— messages, he seems to insist, are best left to another medium. These flirtations with a domestic Fabulism are first and foremost aesthetic experiences. Highly coded scroungings from the psychic attic, their allegiance is not to the unconscious but to the subconscious. They are not hostile to the nostalgic impulse, but they are not respectful of it either."

18

Christopher and Sarah flew to San Francisco that summer for the wedding of Joanne Wells and David Small. After the wedding they rented a car and drove down through Big Sur to Carmel where they stayed for a week. Overwhelmed by his sense of the place— its natural beauty, its boutique elegance, the sea— Freeze spent hours every day sketching.

(EXCERPTS FROM THE UNPUBLISHED JOURNALS OF CHRISTOPHER FREEZE)

Heard from Safadi today that Tompkins has decided to buy *Autumn's Spell*. I'm pleased because I need the money and displeased because I don't think Tompkins really likes the picture and I would rather it went to someone who did.

I suppose I can understand painting a picture I didn't like. (There is Endicott, for example. He paints pictures he doesn't like all the time. He keeps them rather than scrape them down because he has an almost demagogic faith in himself. He is "Endicott the Artist." If he paints something he doesn't like he excuses himself immediately. He accepts it not as something flawed, but as something he simply doesn't understand.) But I can't really understand buying a picture you don't like unless it is just some sort of investment gamble. Buying a picture because you think you should—that suggests a suspiciously incongruous vulnerability to the judgment of others.

❖

It is impossible as a painter or photographer not to be seduced by nature—not to be rendered a drooling perpetrator of clichés.

❖

Went off to the movies with Tim Gold, one of Shield's newest acolytes. We saw *Shipping News*—a tired version of Annie Proulx's novel starring the usually interesting Kevin Spacey and the always alluring Julianne Moore.

❖

Like Sarah, Monica takes an undiscriminating interest in the people around her. She will talk to anyone. Just the other day she got into a long conversation at the grocery store with the woman in line in front of her. This woman—whose name, it turns out, was Annette—told her a story about a neighbor stealing her cat. According to Annette, this neighbor took the cat home, changed its name from Pounce to Georgina, and would not give it back. Annette called the police, and the neighbor called a lawyer. The lawyer the neighbor called put a lien on the cat (apparently you can do that in this state), which they then foreclosed on at a hurry-up auction. This, of course, led Annette to get a lawyer of her own, and just yesterday—after a year and a half of unrest and wrangling—a settlement was reached and Pounce, it seems, was miraculously restored.

❖

Studio. AM. The wee-est of the wee hours. It's just me, Wally, a blazing space heater, and the sound of a far-off garbage truck.

❖

In Thornton's recent work chance has been playing a larger and larger part. I like chance theoretically, and I like to include allusions to it in my stuff—some dripping here, smudging there, the stray splotch—but I rarely care for it being the sole focus. I like pictures to be controlled by the artist. When that control is relinquished for whatever reason, I like it to be relinquished judiciously.

❖

At one time or another Safadi has given most of us on his roster advances against future work. He always wishes it could be more—in part because he is a good man, but mostly I think for business reasons: he would like us all lashed to him for the duration.

❖

Had a visitor named Jordan Seabrook in the studio today. Safadi sent him. Slight, French-looking—he reminds me of someone, but I can't think who. He was a nice enough man, but obviously not very experienced in making these sort of intrusions. He seemed to think I did this all the time—opened the studio to strangers—and that I enjoyed it. I think he was surprised that I wasn't more articulate, more entertaining, more gracious—that I didn't have a stock of fascinating well-practiced stories to tell, that I wasn't going to be carrying the conversational ball. (To carry the conversational ball I need at least half a bottle of wine in me.) I'm sure I was shorter than he expected. (I'm always shorter than they expect. Ask Barnes).

I don't really understand this itch people have to meet the painter. I've never had it myself. I understand maybe wanting to get a glimpse of the guy or of wanting to hear him say a few words (it gives you a sense of who they are, of how honest they are, and, by extension, how honest their work is), but wanting to personally meet, shake hands with, spend time with, talk to—that I don't understand. Painters are best met in the gallery—framed, silent, hanging on the wall.

We talked for an hour—mostly about the half-done thing on my easel, but a little about Safadi and a little about the athletic shoe business. I'm sure it was obvious to Mr. Seabrook that he wasn't dealing with one of those naturally sociable souls, but that didn't stop him form hinting around—hinting about the possibility of some sort of dinner sometime maybe. He wanted me to meet Natalie, his wife (or he wanted Natalie, his wife, to meet me). He showed me a photo (emphatic features: wide mouth, long lean nose, eyes set far apart). She is a newspaper reporter who specializes in crime and who was, at that very moment, putting the finishing touches on a blockbuster story about municipal corruption. He thinks if I met Natalie I would like him better. I might. People who meet Sarah like me better.

❖

I try to hide the contrivances even from myself. I want a picture to look and feel unavoidable.

❖

The key to the success of our marriage is the failure of Sarah's parent's marriage. She never expected much, so she has not been as disappointed as she should be by what she ended up with.

❖

Kevin and Hannah *finito*. As K put it: irreconcilable differences.

❖

It is a peculiar exercise to look at your story—insofar as it is located in the facts of your life—and see it as material to be manipulated for dramatic and ultimately commercial purposes.

(EXCERPTS FROM VARIOUS REVIEWS)

"Freeze's work—a carefully composed mix of the real and imagined, the observed and designed—does not so much repudiate the trendy transgressive aesthetic as ignore it. It favors artistic rather than ideological statements."

19

Back home Freeze started work on *Lazy Susan*. He was hoping for a revelation—something that would show him the way, the direction in which his work should be going—but no revelation was forthcoming. It was one momentary answer after another.

With money from the sale of several early paintings to Robert Mendenhall, owner of a small coffee-shop chain, Christopher and Sarah set off for France. They spent a week in Paris and then rented a car. They drove through the chateau country of the Loire Valley, to Mont-Saint-Michel, to Normandy, then up the coast to Honfleur. Captured by the café culture, Freeze was transformed almost overnight from an Anglophile into a Francophile. Half a year at the ocean, half a year in Paris—this is how a life should be lived.

(EXCERPTS FROM THE UNPUBLISHED JOURNALS OF CHRISTOPHER FREEZE)

I love the idea that it is your fault if you find it difficult to respond to dull and drab work. You have missed the profound essence of dullness and drabness

104

and all that it has to say about vividness and excitement. You are a clod. If you just stare at it long enough and are smart enough, you can come up with something exquisitely sophisticated to excuse it.

❖

My thoughts this morning are what Dr. Hatcher would call disorganized.

❖

Safadi had a long talk with Bill Randall the other day about why he hadn't been buying pictures. Basically what it boiled down to was that he had become afraid. Because of what he had been doing before in the way of acquisitions and because of Helen's ceaseless fraternizing, the Randalls had started to hobnob with a new crowd—a readily censorious, art-conscious crowd—and Bill Randall was worried about making some sort of mistake, about buying something that might expose him to an unflattering assessment if not outright ridicule.

❖

Apparently the affair that Alex said didn't mean anything and was over did mean something and had continued. Elizabeth Something-or-Other, the Jane Austen-loving tramp, is pregnant.

❖

I am sitting here in front of another empty canvas

when Sarah calls to tell me that Wally has an eye infection and she is taking him to the vet.

He is a sickly dog, no doubt about it. Gum problems, ear problems, rashes, kennel cough, kidney stones, etc., etc. It's always something. We're always giving him pills, getting him injections, dropping in drops. Now this. I guess I'll just spend the next few hours pretending not to be worried.

❖

I have an idea for a series—a big series—based mostly and loosely on characters, authors, and scenes from various works of literature. Something from Dickens, for example, and Dostoyevsky. Tentative title: *Literary Suite*. These pictures should be related, but as yet I'm not sure how. I'll have to work on them while I'm working on other stuff because they're going to take forever to figure out and longer than forever to get right.

❖

This is the point, isn't it (as I sit here trying to access this thing) when a colorful character appears from out of nowhere to comfort me in my confusion, someone who talks sense to me and makes me feel fortunate because in some horrible way they have had it so much worse than me. A she, I think—someone with a comically improbable name.

❖

I need to let loose, but I can't. I have spent too long not letting loose. By the time I learned how, it would be too late.

❖

Safadi is looking for a new assistant. Colleen wants to cut back on her hours, so he is after someone part-time. It's a tricky business. He doesn't pay anything, and there are no benefits. The odds of his finding what he is looking for are not good.

❖

Sarah woke me last night and accused me of snoring. Told her to go back to sleep, she was dreaming.

❖

I simply don't understand painters seeking input on pictures in progress. I don't want to talk with anyone about what I'm trying to do—about the thises and thats of a thing. The thises and thats are between me and them or between me and me.

❖

Turner is a sad old satyr. His history is one of erections. He is tiresome to all but himself.

❖

Mark and Sophia are going to Hawaii for a week.

107

❖

Barnes wants photos.

(EXCERPTS FROM VARIOUS REVIEWS)

"*Four Dead* is one of those pictures that just feels inevitably right. A sort of narrative montage that comes at its thesis from all sides, it is held together with a formal repetition of perpendiculars and a strategic use of complimentary color. It feels simultaneously both worked-for and found—like a predominantly intellectual idea that was solved intuitively."

(EXCERPTS FROM VARIOUS INTERVIEWS)

KR: How did you come by the Freeze style?

CF: If I were to concede there is such a thing, I would have to say it was an accident that I had unknowingly spent a lot of time preparing for. I tried doing things other more conventional ways, but I was never very comfortable with the results. When I started doing them this way, the way I'm doing them now, it felt right. Of course at first I didn't know what to make of the pictures. I had no idea what anyone else would make of them either.

KR: Your pictures are small in comparison to much of the art being produced by your peers.

CF: Yes, I'm a little suspicious of scale. If you'll allow me a paraphrase: spectacle is the first refuge of a scoundrel. My pictures are the size they are because I have painted them the way I have. They would be fatiguing if they were any larger.

20

Freeze was traumatized like everyone else by the events of September 11. He did little or no work for several months. He had always maintained some sort of hope for the future, however feeble. This was no longer the case. Learning to live with that was not going to be easy.

(EXCERPTS FROM THE UNPUBLISHED JOURNALS OF CHRISTOPHER FREEZE)

Could there be a bleaker assignment than that of providing an essay for the new Padova show? What can you say about these pictures and maintain your self-respect? You don't want to be on either side of the argument about them—"against" puts you in with the philistines of photo-realism, "for" puts you with the marketplace charlatans of the now.

Monica and Alex are filing for divorce. Neither one of them really wants the kids so they are trying to pass them off on one another. Alex says Monica is more nurturing; Monica says Alex is more capable of providing for their material wants and their educations. Alex is not troubled by the way he feels about J & J; Monica is tormented. We hope Monica prevails, that she will be able to offload these mutants, but we don't think the chances are very good. The courts and Monica's conscience conspire against it.

❖

Received a call today from Susan Duncan at Rock Creek Community College. She wanted to know if I might be interested in taking a teaching position. I was flattered, of course, but my immediate, almost reflexive, response (which I tried to slow down and make sound considered and reluctant) was to say no. It would be nice to make ends meet for a change, to have some regular money coming in, to have some actual health insurance, but I don't have a proselytizing or pedagogical bone in my body and I'm afraid the diversion of time, energy, and attention would get in the way of my doing what I am trying to do. Having a regular job in a regular job-like setting with regular job-like responsibilities would probably be good for me personally—but what is good for me personally probably isn't good for my art, which seems to require a certain sort of intense, monomaniacal focus. What sort of focus could I maintain with classes to prepare for and conduct, with final exams to give and grade, with faculty meetings, with student/teacher conferences? How many hours a day can I spend looking at crap without being affected if by nothing else, then by the lost opportunity to spend that time looking at something good or great—the stuff that feeds me.

It would be nice to be surrounded by people who cared about what I did and thought it was important—people who cared about art and painting. But what would I really have to offer other than my enthusiasm? What I know—or what I know that is valuable and cannot be learned from any standard elementary textbook—is my own and nontransferable. My "solutions," such as they are, are specific—they couldn't possibly mean anything to anyone but me.

❖

Sometimes I feel uncomfortably obvious—like one of those guys with messed-up hair and a misbuttoned shirt.

❖

The longer I look at this picture the less I understand it. Just a minute ago I knew what was wrong with it, I knew how to fix it. Now I have no idea. What I knew a minute ago came and went like a flash—now the whole thing is just a jumble of twists and turns. I can feel it moving away from me—the distance between us is growing greater and greater. Soon it will be someone else's picture. I should time it. Maybe if I focused on the left-hand corner—maybe that would help. Maybe that is the corner that was right. There is nothing more ultra than ultramarine, but is it too much? Is it simply pretty? Does its lower-than-the-highest-common-denominator appeal distract from the seriousness of the less-loveable center? What if all my corners looked like this? I try to meet it halfway, but it won't be met so it is back to the thing as a whole, back to the inscrutable sum, back to a search of my moth-eaten memory.

❖

Cooley is just getting started, but he has it. Wish him good health, a loving wife, and money.

❖

Michelle says if she were in a position to choose—which she isn't—she would rather stay home tonight. She would prefer to curl up on the couch with a handful of video rents, but she has promised Liz (who says celibacy is ruining her personality) to try a little harder—so there he is, on his way, someone named Brandon Waugh, the latest in a long line of doomed experiments.

❖

In the past two days I have forgotten my license plate number, where I put my reading glasses, when Mother's Day is, how many times I've been on an airplane, who played Daisy Buchanan in the movie version of *The Great Gatsby*, and what "objurgate" means. Maybe I should mention this to Dr. Hatcher.

❖

Barnes has a strange sense of entitlement. He thinks I owe him something because he has chosen me as his subject.

(EXCERPTS FROM VARIOUS REVIEWS)

"Much of Freeze's earlier work focused on land and cityscapes, and there are a couple of excellent examples of the genre in this show. 'Back Yard,' for instance, with its explosive, tentacled red tree—a Fauvist picture if ever there was one—highlights the heavy and persistent influence of Matisse.

In turn, 'Neighbor's Fence' with its mauves and grays is a perfect example of the new direction in which Freeze's landscapes seem to have been heading lately: more abstract, using simpler forms and larger areas of undifferentiated color and mass, they seem the product of some sort of distillation process, the boiling down of various responses to their most basic elements.

However different his approaches to the material—conceptual, perceptual, or something in-between—Freeze's animated, painterly paintings share a common virtue: they have the ability to stay alive on the wall long after lesser work has turned to decoration."

21

The attention Freeze was starting to get—the shows, the commissions, the retrospectives—came with all sorts of time-consuming obligations. He was used to only seeing a few people and only when he chose. Now they were everywhere. He had a hard time adjusting.

(EXCERPTS FROM THE UNPUBLISHED JOURNALS OF CHRISTOPHER FREEZE)

What is it I think I'm doing with this picture? Do I know? Yes—pretty much. But can I explain it to anyone? No—which is a good thing because if I could, I'd be tempted to do it and that would be a mistake. Wallace Stevens wrote a poem about placing a jar on a hill in Tennessee. He said, "The wilderness rose up to it/And sprawled around, no longer wild." It—the jar—"took dominion everywhere." That is what an explanation does—it takes dominion. It gathers up the work around it. It steps in front of the thing— whatever it is.

❖

Monica is now officially seeing someone. His name is Edward Becker. He is some sort of itinerant filmmaker who lives in the country and has five dogs. Monica is afraid of the country—it is full of insects and things that want to devour her. She is also afraid of dogs—they aren't as clean as they look, and even the best of them lives a strange and unfathomable life: easygoing and happy one minute, aggrieved and savage the next.

❖

The Randalls called Safadi yesterday. They had decided they wanted to buy *Haze Harbor*, the Anderson picture that Charles had shown them two or three months ago. He had to tell them it was gone—picked up by another less dilatory, less conflicted collector. As you can imagine, they did not take the news well.

❖

I must be a masochist. Why else would someone as impatient as me get involved with stuff like this that takes forever?

❖

New record for the date: seven showers.

❖

It's always difficult to listen to Shield talk about Peter Yeager, his dealer. I've tried, but I just can't take the guy seriously. I see him asleep in front of the television surrounded by porno mags and beer cans.

❖

Have finished the *Literary Suite* series. There are eighteen pictures, all different sizes—or there were eighteen. Now there are actually twelve. I've tossed out six for six different reasons. For instance, I tossed out #9 because it had no reason of its own—it was just there to fatten the show and to keep #8 and #10 from bumping into one another.

I tossed out #5 because it was too small and its tone was wrong—too frivolously satiric. And I tossed out both #17 and #18 because there wasn't enough in either one of them—they simply met the eye.

I tossed out #3 because of the unfortunate auto-biographical references and #13 because it seemed like nothing more than a paraphrase of #12.

I can't make up my mind about #4, which is overly dense and recursive, but I just happen to like about two-thirds of; and #16, which I suspect might be better than I think, but for some reason I just can't really "see" right now.

It's not easy—this falling heroically between the cracks, this making sure you are too mainstream to be regarded as experimental and too experimental to be regarded as mainstream.

❖

Sarah says she believes in signs "occasionally," but I'm not sure she is serious. I think she simply wants to believe in them. She is, after all, more otherworldy than me.

117

❖

I played some poker at Swanson's a couple of weeks ago. It was his regular Thursday night game with his regular bunch of down-and-out buddies. I was welcomed because I was with Tim Gold, who they knew pretty well. He vouched for me as a right-thinking sort of person. I won a little so was emboldened to try again last night. I lost my shirt. This morning I am working on a small still life titled *Poker Table* (lots of cadmium green). If Safadi prices it right, I should be able to break even.

❖

The trouble with Hazlet is his sense of humor—he doesn't really have one. He can try if he feels obliged, but he is much more comfortable being grim and significant and treating people like me (probably rightly) as fools.

❖

I had what I guess you would have to call a dizzy spell today. I've never had one before. I was in the studio working away on the *Books* picture when suddenly the place just started spinning. I felt like I was on some sort of amusement park ride. I had to lie down on the floor (which, of course, I immediately wished I'd swept a little more regularly). I was there for probably half an hour. I thought I was going to have to call someone.

Sarah wants me to see a doctor, but I'm holding

off. I told her I would see one if it happened again, but at present I was inclined to treat the occurrence as enigmatically unique.

❖

I should look into Barnes's bankroll. One thing a subject should know is just how good his biographer's finances are. If the biographer needs money (son going to college, mother into assisted care, new roof on the house), you are in trouble. There is no telling how lurid your story will get. If nothing else, there will be pages and pages about your sex life.

(EXCERPTS FROM VARIOUS REVIEWS)

"Technically there are few painters working with greater facility than Freeze—consider the controlled chaos of his brushstroke, the manipulations of mass, the updated take on old-school modeling. But the special power that sets these pictures apart—what makes them so compelling, what makes them more than simple assertions of an idiosyncratic perception, however gorgeous—is something that comes from somewhere else. It is something that comes from that subtle extra, the infamous X factor—that strange, unaccountable, un-pin-downable, *a priori* magic that is at the heart of artistic instinct."

22

The Freezes bought a house in the fancy-schmantzy suburb of Forrest Heights—an updated Craftsman-style place with a big front porch. After so many years of city living, the sound of lawn sprinklers and crickets (as opposed to garbage trucks and drunks) took some getting used to.

It was that fall when Freeze got caught up in the semi-famous Baker Museum debacle. A scheduled exhibition there was cancelled—an exhibition that would have meant a great deal to Freeze's reputation—when remarks he made about the patently mawkish character of so many of the museum's recent exhibitions made it into the press.

(EXCERPTS FROM THE UNPUBLISHED JOURNALS OF CHRISTOPHER FREEZE)

Edward took Monica over to meet Paul Vaughn, a friend who lived nearby. Paul makes movies too—not as good as Edward's, but bigger budgeted and more successful. Paul thinks everything he says or does is interesting because he is a movie maker and it's him who is saying or doing it or because the people he is saying it to or doing it with are famous or nearly famous— beautiful people with plastic breasts, bleached teeth, unlimited access to certain recreational drugs. They were invited, E & M, to the screening of a rough-cut version of Vaughn's new movie, *The Cruise*—death and mayhem onboard a luxury liner. It is scheduled to open next month.

According to Monica, the lead actor (an ex-male-model) tried to do as much of the movie as he could in profile—believing, obviously, that his right side was his good side. It wasn't. Afterwards, when they had a glass of wine, Monica tried to find something nice to say. The best she could do was a remark on the lavishness of the buffet breakfast scene where Mr. Profile first meets Miss Pillow Lips.

Just read a review of my new show by Roger Denby. He is a serious, heavy-duty academic writing for *The Painting Experience*—a man more frequently focused on bigger fish. (The piece he did just before this one was on Mondrian and just before that on Marcel Duchamp.) He is obviously smart, and he cares about art—but like most of these guys, I don't think he could write a simple declarative sentence if his tenure depended on it. He's pretty good about avoiding the usual nonsense, but he is as conventional as a cop when it comes to covering his ass with equivocating qualifiers.

❖

If only I could think about it later, but I can't. I can't think about anything later. If I'm thinking about something, I continue to think about it. I think about it and think about it. I can't stop. I'll try to stop, but I won't be able to. I'll try to take a few minutes—have a cup of coffee, read something, call Sarah at work— then come back to it, whatever it is, but it never really needs coming back to because it has never really been gone. It has been there with me the whole time like some plaguing taste or smell.

I heard from Safadi that there is another would-be monographer on the scene—someone from an even smaller, more disreputable school than Barnes. His identity is a mystery. I am waiting for him to make himself known to me. The rumor is that he's a crackpot and writes unconventionally

I've been studying Palmer's picture, *Rainbow*— which is supposed to be a painting about a painting he couldn't paint—and I'm having a terrible time. Palmer is so persistently—one might say, insistently— irritating that I have to stop thinking about him every ten minutes or so and do something else. I've complained to Sarah about it. I told her I had become so desperate for a distraction that I had started playing around with the idea of doing a piece about the experience—a painting about a painting about a painting. She said it sounded like a truly excellent idea, but I think she was being facetious. She can be wickedly dry sometimes.

❖

Donaldson wants us to think his stuff is daring because he has peppered it with topical references. To me it just seems easy and opportunistic.

❖

I'm contemplating a set of pictures done from various tortured perspectives.

❖

It's very dispiriting to think that my best chance of finding a larger audience is to be paired with Kaplan and Weber. I don't like their work at all, but it seems a few genre-happy journalists are trying to make a "school" of us.

❖

Barnes wants to talk to me about a part-time job I once had at Kentucky Fried Chicken. I don't know exactly how he found out about this, but I can tell from the excitement in his reedy little voice that he thinks he is onto something. I can hear the thesis forming—Freeze, at the age of fourteen, traumatized by his experiences with a deep-fat fryer, his world

123

view forever altered by an encounter with the tactile and olfactory nightmare of the grease trap.

(EXCERPTS FROM VARIOUS REVIEWS)

"Like all good painters Freeze has remained on the move. Refining, experimenting—he continues to explore his own private piece of aesthetic territory. Over the past couple of years his subjects have changed, his vantage point has changed, his palette has changed. What hasn't changed is his ability to create pictures of great depth and beauty, pictures that produce a spooky sort of emotional immediacy— an immediacy so palpable it can almost be weighed. What hasn't changed is his ability to produce pictures that are, in their simple truthfulness, profound."

23

With the success of the exhibition in New York came a ceaseless number of requests for interviews.

In September Christopher and Sarah took a trip to Washington, D.C. It was their first visit to the nation's capitol. They sat in the Senate Gallery and listened to Gordon Smith speak passionately and hypocritically about the elemental right of *habeas corpus*.

(EXCERPTS FROM THE UNPUBLISHED JOURNALS OF CHRISTOPHER FREEZE)

The Randalls have announced that they are going to go with another dealer. In a malicious act of revenge on all parties, Safadi suggested they try Robert Cloth.

❖

Sarah's body is always warm while mine is cold—especially my hands and feet. When we get in bed at night she wraps me up in her arms and legs so that I too will be warm. This is wonderful in the winter and often in the fall. It's a little less wonderful in the summer.

❖

Bang! It's there. The whole thing. You have to understand that about a painting. It's not like a novel or a movie or your favorite song. Those things all take time. There is no time with a picture. Bang! It's there. The whole thing. You can spend however long you like trying to sort out the how or why of it, but what it is, it is immediately. If one is good enough or lucky enough to get it right, this frozen vortical moment will live on past its freezing. If one gets it right it will persist as an object of interest.

❖

Unfortunately, the older Sarah and I get, the more we seem inclined to help each other drive.

❖

The trouble with Campbell is that he is painting for one man—his dealer, Beasley. He does what he does in large part to please him. Commercially it's smart, but artistically it has been calamitous.

❖

What do you do with someone whose favorite color is yellow?

❖

Good reviews. Good sales. I am free now to worry about becoming part of the establishment.

❖

Timothy Ash wrote a long piece in *Artquake* on the Raymond Wright show. It surprised everyone because it was positive, and because Wright isn't very well known and Ash—who has been around for a while and is one of the revered dinosaurs of the discipline— writes mostly about the big shots. I sort of like him sometimes—but mostly I don't. He has a narrow view of what is good, a strong bias in favor of old-fashioned realistic representation, and an annoying admiration for his own authority. I like the way he takes painting seriously, but too often he takes it too seriously. He can't sit quietly in front of a picture and enjoy it—he has to be perpetually tallying demerits and pasting together proclamations.

Nobody knows for sure why he chose the Wright show, but theories abound. He has been taking a lot of heat lately about his conservatism, about his not getting it anymore, about his not being friendly enough to the avant garde, and I think he chose Wright as some sort of first step in answering these charges. The show is called "Memoir." It's a sort of graphic autobiography. In his piece, Ash used the phrase "a majestical comprehension of aloneness." There is some aloneness to be found in the pictures for sure, but where did "majestical" come from? There is nothing "majestical" here. "Majestical" is ten times too much. Ash must have been in a hurry. He says Wright is never boring when, in fact, he is—half the time at least. The recurring parent portraits are clunky, amateurish slabs of narrative exposition. They're stilted, unbelievable, tiresome. A quarter of the way through you start skipping them. Ash stepped out on a critical limb and said some of the show was probably a bit more conventional than it had to be, but I don't think he is fooling anyone with these toothless demurs. We know where his sympathies lay, and we're always going to take that into account.

❖

Dinner last night at a place whose name I have already forgotten—*tres* continental. Dark, full of morose-looking young men. Felt right at home. Ordered absinthe.

❖

Alan Barnes is looking for enemies. He knows it is from enemies that one hears things—things he can spend pages proving or disproving.

(EXCERPTS FROM VARIOUS REVIEWS)

"And, of course, there is his green. Cezanne had one, Chagall had one, El Greco had one. Freeze has one, too—a green you associate with him. He uses it to beautiful effect in his landscapes, but it pops up in his city pictures and figurative work as well. Rich, cool, comforting—it makes you want to look into the literature on the subject to see exactly what sort of psycho-spectral hocus-pocus is going on here."

A PAINTER'S LIFE

(Excerpts from various interviews)

AK: Why do you paint?

CF: Really?

AK: Yes.

CF: Well, I guess I paint because I have to. I feel lost and deeply depressed when I don't. There was probably a time in my life when I might have been able not to paint, to do something else and be happy, but that would have been a long long time ago. Maybe somewhere in my early teens. Since then I have had to. Looking into why I have to would be a mistake, I think.

24

That winter Freeze started a new group of paintings based on childhood memories. He was being courted by a number of galleries, but he was never really tempted. He painted little and slowly and felt a deep allegiance to Charles Safadi, the man who had given him his chance.

(Excerpts from the unpublished journals of Christopher Freeze)

Sarah's feet are sacrosanct. She is terrified by the idea of a pedicure.

Maybe I should add another piece to the *Literary Suite*—a history painting, a history of the series that includes references to the deleted pictures. Maybe I can work in my worry about #4, about its singular tone and arduous complexity—put together some sort of smorgasbord of subliminal signage to help point the way through this tangle of intuitive speculation.

❖

What else can I say about Jeffrey Nicholson—he is the sort of person who thinks his occasional use of cocaine makes him interesting.

❖

There are times when I see a picture so right that it actually makes me shiver. It will say something perfectly that I could never say myself—not on my best day. All I can hope to do is learn from it.

❖

I wonder if Dr. Hatcher has ever been threatened?

❖

There is a generous side to Safadi in that he would like to see big things happen for me. He is always wanting to introduce me to someone a little further up the food chain, and I am always having to protest. I'm not interested in being introduced to the guy who will introduce me to the next guy who will introduce me to the guy after that—the guy who just might be in a position to do something significant for me. What little energy I have is going into the pictures—there is nothing left to put into a career.

❖

Sometimes when you listen to the shit people talk about art, it makes you want to be a podiatrist.

❖

One of Shield's students is the daughter of Sarah's boss. She paints dogs, cats, and birds. She is best with dogs (German Shepherds, in particular) and okay with cats. The birds—well, the less said about them the better. Shield ignores her, which is a surprise. There was a time not too long ago when he would have kicked someone like her out of his class—sent her off to the coddling Kathy Phillips—but now, new and improved (chastened by a cruel and uncaring omneity), he will periodically try to make the world a better place by going out of his way to not be himself.

❖

Sometimes when I'm stuck on a picture I will focus on colors. If I can get one or two in the right place I can usually find my way to the next taunting impasse.

❖

Spent the evening with the Tuckers drinking wine and looking at their pictures of Paris. They were there for a week and had a wonderful time. They just couldn't seem to stop talking about it. They stayed in the Montparnasse area in a hotel that had once housed Samuel Beckett. John said every morning he woke up hoping to be a little smarter, but to no avail—a fact that Janet was readily willing to confirm. They made me homesick for the place.

❖

132

Had to give a little painting presentation yesterday. Sheer agony.

❖

Another review talking about the drama in my work, but missing the point. That drama—such as it is—is not between contesting emotions so much as it is between contesting ideas about the significance of contesting emotions.

❖

Have been fiddling around half-heartedly with the idea of selling this fancy-schmantzy house and moving back downtown where we both know we belong. The problem, of course, is money. We don't have enough of it. The house—which isn't worth nearly as much as it was a year ago because of the economy—would be difficult to unload because the market is glutted right now. Also, we have gotten accustomed to having a little room to roam around in and, as a consequence, have developed a pretty severe case of square-footage issues when it comes to assessing an alternative. The prospect of getting bunched up again in something small doesn't sit well—especially with Sarah. We haven't figured out the math yet, a way to convince ourselves that paying 1/3 more for 1/2 less would be the right thing to do— but I'm sure we could if we wanted to.

❖

Just finished a new picture and am suffering the

usual post-partum depression. A sort of heavily monkeyed-with montage, I'm still not sure how I feel about it. I was going to call it *The Selling of My Shadow*, but I think I've changed my mind. I'm leaning towards something simpler—*A Painter's Life*, perhaps?

I was on the phone with Barnes the other day. I told him I had to go, that Sarah and I were off to the grocery store. He wanted to know if he could have a copy of the shopping list. As an act of penance I sent him one:

bananas
yogurt
apples
2 spaghetti dinners
2 Szechwan chicken dinners
paper towels
kleenex
garbage bags
cheese
chicken broth
tomatoes
ice cream
tea
crackers
coffee
orange juice
rice
sugar
eggs

(EXCERPTS FROM VARIOUS REVIEWS)

"Freeze's work falls neatly within the parameters of a new tradition that honors an old art—an art that insists the picture, not the wall plaque, do the talking. Elegant, energetic, it stands in diametric opposition to the primitivist aesthetic that has, in one form or another, held sway for so long—an aesthetic that milked an illusory innocence (or esoteric torment) for its authority. In its meticulousness, its precision, its unapologetic display of hard-won virtuosity, Freeze's work asserts the classical virtue of craft. It insists by example that a picture can be beautiful, modern, and serious all at the same time."

25

In March Freeze attended an awards ceremony in Astoria. Normally he avoided these things, but this particular event provided an excuse for he and Sarah to spend a few days at the Cannery Pier Hotel.

The evening's celebration was an ordeal for Freeze. He drank to make it less so. In the early hours on his way back to the hotel with his wife—on a dark and curving stretch of road—Freeze crossed the highway centerline and hit a logging truck head on. Sarah and the driver of the truck were uninjured. Christopher was concussed.

(EXCERPTS FROM THE UNPUBLISHED JOURNALS OF CHRISTOPHER FREEZE)

There is a certain amount of time you can spend with a picture—time in which you continue to discover it. After that, the time you spend with it is time you spend discovering yourself.

❖

I'm supposed to have some ideas this morning,

but I don't. The only thing I can think of is nothing. What sort of something can I make of that?

❖

William Wood came by. He is giving me piano lessons in exchange for a couple of paintings. He has incredible patience—I don't know how he does it. If I played like he did and had to listen hour after hour to someone who played like me, I would go insane.

❖

An interesting thing happens to a painter when he gets picked up by the Shawn Gallery: his paycheck grows, his audience grows, but he doesn't—not in the way he would have if he had not been picked up by them. He invariably ends up doing whatever it takes to stay on the roster, to remain one of the chosen.

❖

I have been coming to this journal more often lately—writing things down, trying to understand what happened to this last picture. I don't suppose there is any difference between what happened to it and what happened to the dozen before, but it feels like there is. Every picture starts off good, but this one started off gooder than most. It was pure promise. I let myself get my hopes up, so it was hard when it fell apart.

Writing about it hasn't helped at all.

❖

Lazlo's work is better in theory than in practice. Hope just the opposite can be said of mine.

❖

The list of painters I would rather be than the one I am is long and mostly distinguished. There is Chardin, for example. Who in their right mind wouldn't want to be him for a while? Look at the still lifes. Who could get more out of less? To paint pictures that instantly transcend their subjects, pictures whose effects are unaccountable, pictures that move you in a way you can never adequately explain—that would be truly wonderful.

❖

I read an interview Christopher Biddenger did the other day. I hated finding out that he relied heavily on his dealer's critiques when it came to shaping a picture. There are so many things it is just better not to know.

❖

I received a letter from a woman named Virginia Wagstad. She wanted to know why I didn't just paint a nice, regular bowl of fruit once in a while. She said she and her friends were tired of having to look at a bunch of Mopey Mike stuff.

❖

When the time comes, I don't want to be there for it. I want to be somewhere else—somewhere far away.

❖

The first thing I ask of a picture is that it be genuine. If it can cross that threshold then my personal feelings about it (liking it or disliking it, for instance) become considerably more interesting and complex.

❖

Kevin wants me to introduce him to Michelle.

(EXCERPTS FROM VARIOUS REVIEWS)

"Freeze shows no interest in the grim symbolic stuff that has been getting so much attention lately—which, of course, is one of the things you just have to love about him. While his view of human nature is clearly existential, it is not so clearly bleak. His landscapes are alive with menace and his cityscapes alive with anxiety, but somehow they have managed to steadfastly eschew the commonplace moral gravity favored these days by both jurors and curators."

26

In May, still suffering side effects from his accident, Freeze was checked into a clinic at the Providence Medical Center.

(EXCERPTS FROM THE UNPUBLISHED JOURNALS OF CHRISTOPHER FREEZE)

Absurdist, surrealist, something-ist—they are always trying out labels on me. They are always trying to gloss what is basically just a wanton cockamamieism.

❖

If a picture works it will be convincing—you will have to look at it a long time before you start to care about how it was made.

❖

Monica came by last night all excited about her new adventure. She is going to be in one of Edward's movies—a live-action short titled *The Visit*. She is going to play the wife of an institutionalized mental

140

patient (no stretch there—not after Alex). The story opens with her making one of her regular trips to the booby hatch. Dylan, the husband, has had a psychotic break. He does not recognize his wife. She has told him who she is a half-dozen times, but he does not believe her. He thinks this woman, this "Kayla," is posing as his wife, that she is some sort of actress, some sort of secret agent who has been sent to gather information about him—information that will be used to keep him locked up.

❖

Was introduced to a man at Safadi's by the name of Patrick Moreland. He collects my work. Voluble, sure of himself—he explained several of my pictures to me.

❖

Bayless says he follows a star—me, if I follow anything, it's a thunderstorm.

❖

Bought a small figure painting by Ryan Rhodes— a Rembrandtesque thing done in blacks and browns titled *Woman in a Grotto*. A tiny but talismanic piece, it protects a place in the living room (and in my day) and makes me deeply happy.

❖

I haven't really decided yet how I feel about this

neurologist—the heavily credentialed, semi-famous, ex-Australian Dr. Arnold Bagley. He is pleasant enough and has a good handshake, but there is something distinctly alarming about the amount of work he has been willing to put into making himself look like Santa Claus.

❖

Sarah is a natural nurse.

❖

It would be nice to believe for a little while that it was not all just a matter of luck.

(EXCERPTS FROM VARIOUS REVIEWS)

"The inner logic of Freeze's cryptic, disoriented goo-fest becomes clear early in the exhibition. A first-glance sense of randomness resolves itself quickly as the pictures coalesce (more or less) around a classic tripartite structure. Flattering the scatter, they can be read as the artist's response not only to numbing familiarity, but to contemporary social and psychological dislocation."

(EXCERPTS FROM VARIOUS INTERVIEWS)

GH: What are you working on now?

CF: Something not completely different, but different

enough, I think, to make you wonder if maybe it was by someone else.

GH: And that is a good thing?

CF: I don't know. I suppose that will depend on your point of view.

LaVergne, TN USA
19 December 2009
167613LV00002B/228/P